To Jenn 0

Snow Effect

By
Liana Garson

Stay Warm!

Liana
Dana
Garson ♡

ISBN (print): 978-1-945075-24-7

DEDICATION

To my boys…
Once-in-a-lifetime love is a real thing.
Wait for it.

ACKNOWLEDGMENTS

I simply cannot publish another book without saying "thank you" to both Rhenna Morgan and Lauren Smith. I'm grateful for our monthly lunches (with you too, Jaci Burton!) and for your words of support and comfort. Without the two of you to lean on, get advice from, share experiences and commiserate with I'd probably go stark raving mad in this topsy-turvey world we authors choose to live in.
hugz

CHAPTER ONE

"I'm about to lose what little grip I have left on my sanity," Nicole Cartwright whispered into the telephone.

"What are you talking about, girl?" Charlotte Manning, Nicole's grandmother and most favorite person in the world, asked. "Things can't be that bad."

"Wanna bet?"

"Believe me, what seems like a big deal now will only be a speck in your memory when you get to be my age. If you're lucky enough to remember the speck, that is. So, what's wrong with my baby girl?"

Nicole watched the reason for her irritation swish past her desk, leaving a cloud of perfume in her wake. Yvonne Brinkley, the entertainment newscaster, headed for the boss's office. Again. Gritting her teeth, Nicole growled into the phone, "I'll tell you about it over lunch."

"Sure thing, hon. You sure you'll make it until then?"

"I think so."

"I'm willing to listen now if you need to talk about it. No sense in ruining your morning over a bit of angst."

"Yeah, I know." Nicole rummaged through the papers scattered across her desk to avoid watching Yvonne from the corner of her eye. The annoying newscaster wore a hot-pink suit that glared in contrast against the drab gray cubical walls. Her bleached blonde hair and over-tanned skin, combined with the brightly colored suit, created something akin to a train wreck. The average Joe just couldn't help but stare.

There had to be some fashion rule about not wearing hot pink in the middle of winter.

Just then Nicole noticed the note she had scribbled on the corner of her desk calendar. "Oh! I forgot to tell you. Steve is going to meet us for lunch. I hope you don't mind."

"Steve? I haven't seen that naughty boy in almost a month. Of course I don't mind," Charlotte exclaimed.

Steve Leverton was Nicole's best friend. They met in college. Around that same time Steve had an identity crisis over his sexual preferences. Nicole had been there for him and supported him through the emotional highs and lows. Steve held her hand when her father died. Ever since, they cried on each other's shoulders and kept each other company—and sane—at all family functions.

Nicole grinned. "I didn't think you'd mind."

Every time they were together, Steve flirted outrageously with Nana Charlotte. Nana loved Steve's attention and flattery. He was the only person Nana tolerated that kind of behavior from. Anyone else she would pin to the wall with a stare while informing them that they were full of malarkey.

Charlotte sighed. "You know, it's a shame to waste such a fine specimen of a man."

"I know, Nana. It is," Nicole agreed.

"Oh well." Charlotte's wistful voice brightened. "I'll see you in a little while. Camille's Deli, right?"

"Yup. At noon sharp." Nicole added, "Love you."

"Love you too, hon."

Just talking to Nana loosened the knot of tension that had gathered between Nicole's shoulder blades. The same place Yvonne would probably stick that proverbial knife if she ever got the chance. All so she could get her claws on Nicole's spot, *Art at Dark*.

Art at Dark had been Nicole's brainchild from when she worked as an intern under Yvonne. It focused on local artists, gallery openings, and premieres as a way of promoting the arts in the community, and it fit with the mayor's plan to grow that part of town. Nicole never dreamed the spot would become as popular as it had in the last year.

It came as no surprise that Yvonne wanted control of it. Instinctively she knew Yvonne would ruin the show.

Nicole spent the next hour and a half playing keep-away from Yvonne. It was cowardly, but best for everyone if she stayed away. The temptation to tell Yvonne what she thought of her attempts to control everyone, most especially other reporters' areas of expertise, grew daily. Once she got started, it would be a short leap to telling Yvonne exactly what she thought of her on a personal level. And *that* wouldn't do at all.

Hence the reason she continued to duck behind file cabinets then sneak out the back door to escape for lunch before being cornered.

A couple of hours with her two favorite people should level out her attitude. Charlotte and Steve were already seated at a table when she arrived. Just seeing them drained some of her tension.

Steve stood when she reached the table. "There you are." They exchanged quick kisses on the cheeks. "We ordered a raspberry iced tea for you."

"Did you ask for some rum with it?" she asked.

He winked. "We'll save that for happy hour."

Before taking her seat, Nicole draped one arm around Charlotte's shoulder and gave her a squeeze. "I'm so glad to see you guys."

Charlotte squeezed one of Nicole's hands. "I take it your day didn't get any better?"

"Yes and no." She dropped her purse on the floor and plopped into her chair.

"Surely Yvonne isn't still trying to tell you what to do?" Steve asked.

Nicole looked around the restaurant to make sure no one from the office or any of the other stations was nearby. After all, in the news business, you never knew who might be listening. "Of course she is. But she's only part of my problems these days."

"Yvonne is that pushy woman you interned under, right?" Charlotte asked.

Nicole swallowed a drink of tea and nodded. "Afraid so."

The expression on Charlotte's face showed how unimpressed she was with that thought.

Steve cut in before Charlotte could voice her considerable opinion of Yvonne. "Yvonne has made it clear she wants to be a pain in the ass to as many people as possible. You should be used to that."

Nicole took a deep breath. "Yeah, well, between Yvonne and Mom, the only time I get any peace these days is when I'm at the gym and my phone is in the locker on mute."

"Lydia's been giving you grief?" Charlotte looked over the top edge of her menu with a puzzled expression. "She's not still trying to find Mr. Right for you, is she?"

"Got it in one," Nicole exclaimed with false cheeriness. She elbowed Steve when he failed to stifle a groan.

"*I* can't take another of your mother's fix ups." He flopped back in his seat, covered his face with his hand, and shook his head as if in denial, then exclaimed, "Doesn't she realize that by giving out your phone number to anyone and everyone, she might have gotten you a stalker?"

Charlotte startled at that bit of information.

Nicole gave Steve a cross look then tried to soothe Nana's worries. "We don't know that it's a stalker."

Steve ignored her warning look. "Are you still getting flowers and cards from creepy unknown persons?"

Nicole shrugged. "Just a couple more."

Steve raised one eyebrow and held her gaze. His expression made it clear he didn't believe her in the least.

"We don't know that it's someone Mother gave my information to." Nicole scrambled for an excuse.

Steve's expression didn't change.

Charlotte interrupted their stare down by asking, "What are you two talking about?"

Steve answered for her. "Nicole started getting flowers a couple of months ago." With a roll of his eyes, he added, "Cheap, unimpressive flowers like mums, by the way." Then his face turned serious. "It's the cards that are creepy. They've all said something like, 'I'm still watching,' or, 'Can't wait to see you again.'"

Charlotte frowned. "I have to agree with Steve. It is a little strange." She reached across the table and wrapped her hand around one of Nicole's wrists. "Have you told the police?"

"No. I did tell Bob, though. He said reporters often received gifts from viewers but to keep him posted if the cards became threatening in any way."

Charlotte patted Nicole's arm and nodded in agreement. She knew Bob from when he had been just a newspaper-delivery boy. It was one of the advantages of living in a city the size of Springfield. It wasn't a small town, but for those who grew up in the area, it still had a hometown feel. Nicole knew Charlotte trusted Bob's opinion on the matter.

"You could always hire a handsome bodyguard," Nana offered. "Kill two birds with one stone. You'd have a man in your life to make Lydia happy. And you wouldn't have to worry about a potential stalker."

"Oooo." Steve leaned closer. "Get one who looks like that guy on that Viking show. All beefy and rugged and rough looking. One who makes people think he'd rip their arms off instead of having a conversation with them."

"Then send the bill to Lydia." Nana added under her breath, "It'd serve her right for putting you in that kind of position."

Sadly the idea had merit.

CHAPTER TWO

The waitress came to take their orders, cutting off any further talk of Nicole's supposed stalker. As soon as the waitress left, Charlotte graciously diverted their conversation. "So, dealing with Yvonne and your mother is stressing you out," she prompted.

"When you put it that way, it doesn't sound like much. But it's not just Yvonne being Yvonne."

Steve snorted and muttered under his breath, "That alone is enough to drive a saint to drink."

"Yvonne is trying to get *Art at Dark* moved under her spot."

Steve and Charlotte's combined gasps of shock could be heard over the lunch crowd clatter.

"Surely not!" "You must be kidding!" They spoke in unison. If it hadn't been such an uncomfortable topic, Nicole might have laughed at how much alike the two of them were. Maybe that was why she loved them both so much.

"What does Bob think about it?" Charlotte asked.

"I'm not entirely certain." Nicole paused to allow the waitress to set the rolls and butter on their table. As soon as the lady left, all three of them reached into the basket to grab one of the honey-coated crescent roll Camille's was famous for.

"He hasn't said anything to make me think he's planning to move it under her." Nicole took a bite of the warm, flaky roll, letting the slightly sweet taste soothe her worried soul. "But he also hasn't shot the idea down."

Steve harrumphed around a mouthful of bread.

"Bob's smart enough to realize that someone with a degree in art history who can hold an audience's attention without boring them to death is the best choice for the show's spot," Charlotte said with confidence.

"I doubt Yvonne would know the difference between Michelangelo and Beethoven if you spelled it out for her," Steve muttered.

Nicole chuckled then sobered. "The bad thing is, I don't know if I really want to keep *Art* or not."

Steve choked on the bite he had just taken.

Charlotte sat up in her chair. "You can't mean that."

Nicole grimaced. "But I do. I've been having doubts about whether or not I want to keep doing this."

"I thought you loved the station," Steve exclaimed.

"I do and I don't." Nicole struggled to organize her thoughts. "I love doing the research and interviewing artists, and I certainly love going to all the gallery exhibits. But I'm not all that comfortable in front of the camera."

Charlotte nodded her understanding. "You never were a fan of the limelight."

Steve shrugged. "I do have to admit to being surprised when you first told us about doing the show. But you were so excited about it that I thought you'd gotten comfortable with it."

"I did. And I am, on one level. But it always drains my energy to be upbeat and outgoing with so many strangers."

"Add to it a weird 'fan' and you're probably ready to scream, huh?" Steve asked.

Nicole crinkled her nose. "Yeah, kinda."

"How long do you think you have to make up your mind?" Charlotte asked.

"Probably not long. Bob called me into his office today and said he wanted both me and Yvonne to cover the Hartsford Charity Auction."

Steve's eyes lit up. "Ooooo. I heard that was coming up soon. It's supposed to be the hottest ticket in town. Everyone who is anyone is going to be there." He grimaced. "And you have to go with the Joan Rivers of Greene County?"

Nicole nodded. "And somehow get exclusive footage of the auction pieces before the event." She sighed and slumped back in her chair. "If I don't, it'll only fuel Yvonne's argument to control the show and it won't matter if I decide to keep the spot."

Steve and Charlotte made sympathetic noises.

"Well, you know where to find me if you need a date," Steve

teased. "Even if it means putting up with Yvonne's bitchy self."

"I may take you up on the offer to be a buffer zone."

"When is the auction?" Charlotte asked.

"A little over three weeks."

Steve's brow furrowed. "That's barely enough time to find a dress. Maybe we could take a drive to Joplin and go to that little boutique you love so much."

Nicole cringed. She hated the idea of spending money on a dress that may not be worn again. Especially since she'd emptied most of her savings to pay off the loan on her car. But being on camera with a guest list full of Springfield's elite meant she wouldn't get away with wearing something from her closet.

"That's a wonderful idea, Steve," Charlotte exclaimed. "You have such good taste, I'm sure you'll help our girl find just the thing. And it'll be my treat!"

"You don't need to do that, Nana."

"I want to." Charlotte waved one hand in the air. "Pretend it's an early birthday gift."

Steve launched into talk of calendars and which day they could both get away from work, giving Nicole no chance to protest further. By the time the waitress returned with their lunch, they had settled on the Tuesday before the auction. That still gave her a couple days for any alterations she'd need done.

As they finished eating, Nana asked, "You are still planning to go to Rosie and Milton's anniversary party this weekend, aren't you?"

Nicole grimaced. "That's *this* weekend?"

"Yes it is." She waved her fork at Nicole. "Despite the fact that I might be adding to your current stress level, I will remind you that you promised me and Rosie *and* Milton that you'd be there."

Nicole groaned, remembering her promise after missing the last four family functions.

"What anniversary party?" Steve asked between bites of pie.

"It's Rosie and Milton's fortieth and they wanted to get the entire family together to celebrate," Charlotte answered. "You know you are more than welcome to attend, Steve, even though little missy here couldn't be bothered to tell you about it."

"If they invited the whole family, they need a lot of space. Where did they decide to hold it?" he asked.

"At the cabin, of all places," Nicole mumbled.

Steve's brow rose in question. "The cabin?"

"Milton's family has owned a place out on the Lake of the Ozarks for generations," Charlotte clarified. "They have a big bunkhouse that has been renovated over the years. It can hold quite a few people at one time."

Steve looked at Nicole. "Is that the same cabin you told me about? The one you used to stay at for the summer?"

Nicole nodded but didn't say anything more.

"Wasn't it Milton's grandson who—"

"Yup." Nicole abruptly cut Steve off. She took a big gulp of tea to drown the twinge that always came whenever she thought of Randy Stephenson.

"You know... Since you're going to the cabin," Charlotte gave Nicole a look that said she would hear no arguments on the point, "there is something I could use your help with."

"What's that?" Nicole asked.

"And it just might help your show."

Nicole frowned. "You mean *Art at Dark*?" She glanced at Steve to see if he had a clue where Nana was going with the conversation. He just shrugged and shook his head in answer to her unspoken question.

Charlotte nodded and smiled mysteriously. "Would it be beneficial for your show to do a spotlight on a couple of old French paintings? Paintings that have never been in a museum, but might have been painted by a very famous painter?"

CHAPTER THREE

A few days later Nicole tried to wrap up her last broadcast of the week early so she could hit the road ahead of the five o'clock traffic.

"Thanks, Nicole," replied the backup newscaster who covered the weather when the main guy was out sick. "Can't wait to hear more about the Hartsford Charity Auction."

"As soon as we have the details we'll post information on our blog about how our viewers can get involved even if they can't make it to the live auction," Nicole added.

"Excellent. And I hear that you may have some of your own treasures to report on next week as well?"

Nicole looked up at the camera that she knew would still be aimed on her and barely contained her surprise. She'd only told Bob about the paintings, but the worst place to try to keep something quiet was an office full of reporters. "Er... Yes, maybe so."

"Can you give us some hints on what you'll be doing this weekend and where this treasure may be coming from?"

So much for a quick transition between reports, Nicole thought as she struggled to maintain the cheery banter with someone she wanted to smack right now. "This weekend I'll be visiting family. The 'treasure,'" Nicole made quotation marks in the air with her fingers as she spoke, "is a couple of paintings my great-grandmother picked up while touring France years ago. They've been locked away for more than fifty years, so no one remembers what they look like or who painted them." Nicole smiled her best TV smile.

"Sounds exciting."

"I'm excited to learn more about my great-grandmother's travels. I'll be sure to update you when I return on whether or not they're long-lost treasures." Nicole remained in her seat until she got the "all clear" signal from the crew then headed to her work desk.

She had just reached her destination when Bob zipped by in his usual rush. "Great job on the teaser for next week's report, kid."

"Thanks."

Bob stopped at the end of the aisle before turning toward his office. He faced Nicole again and added, "Don't forget to let me know how your treasure hunt turns out as soon as you're back. Got it?"

"Even if it ends up *not* being a treasure?" Nicole asked with a raise of one eyebrow.

"Yup. We still might be able to pull a story out of it anyway."

"Okay," Nicole said, dragging out the word. If anyone could make a story out of some dusty souvenirs, Bob could.

She shrugged to herself and attempted to make order of the paperwork scattered across her desk. She'd worry about the story next week. Right now she needed to clear the piles of paper so she could get on the road. Her car was already packed for the drive to the cabin. Charlotte had suggested she leave immediately after work instead of waiting until morning, since they were forecasting heavy snow in the area.

Now that she'd had a few days to settle in to the idea, she looked forward to a weekend away. It would be good to see some of the family, and she was a little excited by the idea of rummaging around the attic looking for the paintings. As a girl she used to play dress up in the attics as she looked through old photo albums and played with boxed-up trinkets and memories.

A couple of days away from the office and all the politics sounded like heaven on Earth. The thought of dozing in the sauna sounded even better.

Her heart gave a little twist when she remembered the last time she used the sauna at the cabin. Randy had been loving and tender. She thought he had been telling her he loved her, but a couple days later, he left for good.

Nicole shook off the memories. It was too bad she wasn't seeing anyone. It would have been nice to share the weekend. Maybe then she could replace her last memories of Randy with new ones that didn't hurt as much.

She stuffed the last scraps of notes littering her desk into a file labeled as miscellaneous and shoved it into a drawer. As she reached under her desk for her purse and carryall bag, Nicole heard Yvonne's heels clicking on the laminated floor. Her instinct was to grab her things and run, but judging by the sound, she didn't have enough time to make a clean getaway. She resigned herself to dealing with the annoyance that was Yvonne.

"I hope you're planning to use some of your time off to look for a new dress for the Hartford Auction. As charming as that navy cocktail dress is that you wore to the last two gallery openings, you simply can't be seen in it *again*." Yvonne rested one hip on the corner of Nicole's desk. "And you might think about picking something in a brighter color. It would do your complexion a world of good."

Telling herself that Yvonne probably meant well, just came across as a bitch, didn't help Nicole's growing irritation. She dropped her purse and bag on her desk and stood so she wouldn't have to look up at Yvonne.

"No, actually I was planning to go dress shopping next week." Without giving Yvonne a chance to start up about how important the event would be for the station, Nicole continued. "Steve and I plan to drive into Joplin one evening. I'm sure we'll be able to find something suitable."

That seemed to pacify Yvonne. "Well, you do have a figure that allows you to buy most things right off the rack." She shrugged one shoulder and picked at the petals of the flower arrangement Nicole's had received that morning. "Alterations shouldn't be a problem."

Nicole wasn't sure if she should be insulted by that comment or not. She chose to overlook it just like the last fifty pseudo-insults Yvonne had dropped. "I guess some of us are just lucky that way."

"I suppose so," Yvonne murmured.

Nicole removed her keys from her purse and dropped them on the desk as a way of indicating that she was about to leave.

Yvonne might have seen the hint but chose to ignore it. "I heard you're going to visit family this weekend, but I didn't get all the talk about some kind of treasure. What is that all about?"

She knew she shouldn't be shocked by anything Yvonne said or did, but the audacity of the woman still overwhelmed her sometimes. They weren't friends. Why would Yvonne think she would want to sit and chat with her? Much less confide anything in her?

Hoping it would allow her to get away quickly, she waved the question away with one hand. "Oh, it's nothing, really. I don't know how things get so blown out of proportion around here. It's just a couple of paintings my grandmother wants me to take a look at."

"Why did Vince blather on about it being some kind of treasure then?"

"I don't know." Nicole was genuinely puzzled by that. "Maybe he hoped to get some kind of attention for the show."

Yvonne squinted at her as if she were trying to decide whether or not Nicole lied. Finally she said, "Maybe so." She stood then dropped the amethyst cluster she had been handling back on Nicole's desk. "He is a newbie. Well, have a good weekend."

Nicole watched Yvonne walk away, shocked there hadn't been any other insults. Not wanting to take any chances on Yvonne coming back, Nicole grabbed her things and headed to her little Toyota. She started the engine and kicked the heater on.

Early February seldom had more than a handful of days above freezing. The weathermen were predicting a large storm would roll in over the weekend, but she had agreed to go to the party. *Promised* to go, actually. Nana would never forgive her if she didn't. And for Nana alone, she would risk getting snowed in, in a place that held painful memories.

There were a lot of happy memories, too.

She dialed Steve's number, hoping to catch him between meetings. Surprisingly he picked up on the second ring. "Steve Leverton speaking."

"Hey. Are you busy?" Nicole huddled in the driver's seat, trying to keep warm.

"Yeah, but I can spare a few minutes. What's up?" Exhaustion echoed in his voice.

"I was just about to leave and I thought I'd try one more time to talk you into going with me."

"Awww, you know I'd love to go, but I can't. Not this weekend. I've got too much to do to get ready for that big presentation on Monday."

"I know. But I had to try one more time. You probably need

the escape as much as I do."

"That's true." Steve sighed into the phone. "But my break will have to wait a few more weeks."

"If that's the case then maybe you and I could sneak off to the Springfield Spa for the full treatment the weekend after the auction."

"Oooo. We haven't done that in a while, have we?" Steve said wistfully.

"Doesn't it sound great?"

"It does." Steve paused. "I wonder if that sexy massage therapist still works there."

"Did you two ever hook up?" Nicole asked, remembering the tall blond with muscles stacked on muscles.

"Nah. We traded a few emails, but it never amounted to anything."

"That's a shame. He was good looking." She laughed. "I was jealous he wasn't my type."

"Yes, well, you do have good taste in men, dahling."

Nicole laughed. Steve had the best sense of humor. "So do you, babe."

She looked around the parking lot and spotted a familiar figure headed in her direction. She groaned in dismay.

"What's the matter?" Steve asked even though he sounded distracted.

"Ed," Nicole said, sounding as tired as Steve had when he first answered the phone.

"Ed? As in Ed the Pest?" Disdain dripped from Steve's words.

Steve had labeled Ed "the Pest" when he didn't take no as an answer and repeatedly asked Nicole to go out with him. She finally went to Bob in order to get Ed to stop bothering her.

"He spotted me in the parking lot before I could get out of here."

"You're still at work?"

"Yeah. I'm still in the parking lot. I was letting the car warm up a bit."

"Do you want me to call Bob for you? I bet he's still in the office."

"No, it's all right. I can handle Ed," she reassured him. "I keep telling you Ed's mostly harmless, he's just annoying."

"I'm not entirely sure of that," Steve mumbled. "But I do agree with him being annoying."

"I'll be fine. Finish up whatever you need to do so you can go home."

"Okay," he answered reluctantly. "Call me after you get to the cabin so I know you're okay."

Nicole rolled her eyes. "Yes, Mom."

They hung up and Nicole began to rearrange her things in the seat next to her. As expected, Ed walked up and tapped on her window.

"Hey, Nicole."

She took a deep breath and rolled the window down. "What's up, Ed?" She forced her tone to be polite but cool.

"I saw you sitting in your car and I wanted to make sure you weren't having car trouble or anything."

"No. Just making a call before I left." She smiled and left her finger on the button, ready to close the window at her first opportunity.

"I saw your show today," Ed continued.

"Oh?"

"Yeah. You did a good job, like always."

"Thanks." Nicole kept her voice neutral. She didn't want to encourage him, but she didn't want to be rude either. After all, he was the associate producer.

Ed shifted from one foot to the other. "So, are you really going hunting for treasure this weekend?"

Nicole pictured herself slapping Vince, the newscaster. "No. I'm not going hunting for treasure."

"But you said on your show—"

"I know what Vince implied, but it's not the whole story."

"What do you mean?" Ed sounded a little put off.

"I'm not hunting for treasure. My grandmother told me about some old paintings that she had forgotten about until recently." Nicole shrugged. "They may have some value after all these years. But most likely they're just souvenirs from my great-grandmother's travels."

"Oh." Ed sounded disappointed.

"But you never know. I don't remember ever seeing them before, so it's kind of exciting." Feeling some warmth from the car vents, she adjusted the heater controls to turn it up. "A lot of people in the family say I got my love of art from my great-grandmother. She supposedly had exquisite taste, too."

"Well, maybe that will work out after all." Ed's eyes brightened at the prospect.

"I hope so. Hey, I don't want to be rude, Ed but I need to get on the road before the traffic gets bad."

"You're leaving tonight? Before the storm?"

"Yeah. That's another reason I'm in a little bit of a hurry," she added with her best TV smile.

"Oh, gotcha."

"Have a good weekend." Nicole rolled up the window, cutting off their conversation. She put the car into reverse and waved in Ed's direction.

As she pulled out of the parking lot, she glanced in her rearview mirror and saw Ed returning to the office. Shrugging off the thought, she clicked on her MP3 player and turned up the volume. She had a couple of hours of driving ahead of her. With luck the weather would hold off until she reached the cabin.

And maybe Rosie would have some of her homemade hot chocolate prepared when she arrived.

CHAPTER FOUR

Randy Stephenson sighed when his cell phone rang for the tenth time after he left the office. What had he been thinking when he decided to get away for the weekend? Oh, yeah, that it would be nice to see Pop and Gram again and perhaps get a little R&R while he was at it.

At this rate, though, he wouldn't make it across the state line. He'd had to pull the car over three times to look something up on his laptop so his junior associate could finish a proposal they needed for Tuesday. Randy's assistant, Jenny, managed his schedule and appointments like a pro, but had limited computer skills and no idea where to find the information they needed. Jenny was close to retirement age and told him frequently she saw little point in learning any more of those fancy computer things than she had to.

Needing a break more than his juniors needed their hands held, Randy decided to ignore the phone and let it roll to voice mail. It was already after five. If a real emergency had popped up, he'd handle it when he got to the cabin. At this rate it would be midnight when he got there.

It had been years since he'd been to Pop and Gram's cabin. The summers he spent there before his mom had gotten sick had been the last moments of peace and true joy he remembered having.

And there had been Nicki.

His one regret in life.

Ever since his mother died, he'd been determined to make something of himself. It had been a long road, but he had a successful career. A thriving architectural firm he'd built from the ground up along with his best friend, Vince Hewitt. Because his business continued to do well, he was able to live a more-than-comfortable lifestyle in Chicago.

Attracting women had never been a problem for him. Perhaps they just preferred blond hair and blue eyes, but he liked to think his charming personality had something to do with it. The fact that he liked nice things and didn't mind spending money on those he felt were important might also influence some people.

Of course he didn't have a wife or kids to support, so he could justify spending a little more on the car he wanted and on his designer suits. Unlike Vince, who was now expecting a second baby. Not that Vince didn't live well; however, his extra cash went toward family vacations and remodeling the baby's room.

But Vince had something he didn't. He had a family to go home to every night. Someone to comfort him when a deal didn't go the way they had hoped. He even had general direction in life, a purpose, if you will. Randy had his company. The women he dated seemed to be more interested in his lifestyle and his connections than in him. Usually he ran out of polite conversation after a few dates. He'd only been in one serious relationship since Nicki. Thankfully that one ended with both of them acknowledging something was missing and they were better off as friends.

As he drove across the Illinois state line into Missouri, Randy let his mind drift back to the last summer he'd spent at the cabin.

He knew Nicki had been in love with him. She'd told him early that summer. He had been in love with her, too, as much as a twenty-year-old boy could be, but he'd never told her. When his mother had taken ill, he used it as an excuse to rush home before he did something crazy. Like ask Nicki to marry him.

Even at twenty, Randy knew he had nothing to offer her. He and his mom were getting by, but just barely. He didn't want that kind of life for Nicki, so he ran. And, as much as he regretted letting her go, it had been the right decision at the time.

Months of caring for his mom, working a part-time job, and going to college filled his life. There were days when he wanted nothing more than to pick up the phone and call Nicki just to see how she was. By then he figured she hated him for leaving.

He'd told himself she was better off without him. She had gone to college and last he heard from Pop and Gram, she had a successful career with the local news station. She hadn't married yet either. Perhaps she focused on her career in the same way he did on building his business.

Gram and Charlotte were still thick as thieves. Nicole might come to the party with Charlotte. If she did, maybe he'd get a chance to ask her why she'd never married.

Randy picked up his phone and dialed Pop's number. The call rolled to voice mail. He'd been trying to reach them since he left the office but hadn't been able to. If there were many people at the cabin, Pop wouldn't be able to hear his phone ringing. He might have also left his phone in his coat pocket or in another room.

Pop had the landline phone disconnected at the cabin a few years before, when everyone started carrying cell phones. No point in paying for it when they only visited a few weeks out of the year. Cable and internet were unavailable, too. Which made it easy to escape from the modern world.

And, boy, could he use the break right now. He contemplated staying for the rest of the week after the party just to have some peace and quiet. If it weren't for the Halliburton proposal due on Tuesday, he would.

Vince could handle it but he liked to keep tabs on all the major projects. Or, as Jenny recently pointed out, he stayed involved with everything at the office so he didn't have time to think about how lonely he was.

Randy frowned at the long stretch of highway before him. "I'm not lonely. I have lots of friends. I get out and do things." He thought about it for a moment more. "I even talk to myself."

Chuckling, he added, "Maybe I am a little crazy." *See what stress does?*

He drove in silence for several miles then noticed white flecks falling on his windshield. "Great," he mumbled. "I didn't think the snow would blow in for a couple more days. Guess the weatherman was off again."

Randy turned the radio on and flipped stations until he found one playing music he could stand. Maybe the snow would remain light until he made it to the cabin.

CHAPTER FIVE

A couple of hours after leaving the office lot, Nicole turned off the county road onto the gravel drive that led to the cabin. Memories assaulted her. Trees she had climbed as a child. Small streams she had crossed while chasing her cousins. Crawdads they found along the banks. Camping by the lake with the whole family. Roasting marshmallows in the campfire. Taking long walks through the woods, sometimes hand in hand. Making love on the floor near the fireplace of the cabin.

She shook off the image of her and Randy together and the feeling of warmth that went with it. Instead she focused on keeping the car on the winding path. The gravel crunched beneath the tires and the snow fell heavy on the windshield. She had been lucky there had only been a light dusting all the way to the cabin. It appeared she arrived just in time for the weather to create messy driving conditions.

When she navigated around the last bend in the road, the cabin came into view. For some reason, very little light shone through the shaded windows. And there were no cars in the circle drive. Perhaps everyone else parked near the barn behind the cabin. She could move her car later if Milton wanted her to.

She took a moment to absorb the changes to the cabin. There were new windows installed on the front. Rosie must have hounded Milton to change out the old ones. Despite how leaky the old windows had been, Milton never wanted to replace them. He just changed the glass panes if they broke. Bet it hurt his thrifty heart to finally do it.

After parking close to the front porch she unbuckled her seat belt. When she opened the car door, the smell of the lake and pine trees, as well as the cold of the falling snow, permeated her senses. She took a moment to allow the peace and quiet to sink in.

Nana was right about needing to take some time off.

Nicole stacked her bags and the cooler on the porch then returned to her car to gather up the last odds and ends before locking it for the night. *I wonder why no one heard me pulling into the drive?* By now someone should have come to greet her. She climbed the steps to the door then knocked.

There were no sounds coming from inside the cabin. She peeked through the window next to the door but didn't see anyone. The only light seemed to be coming from the kitchen. Using the key Nana gave her in case she arrived after everyone had gone to bed, she unlocked and opened the door then pulled her things into the dark entryway.

Closing the big wooden door behind her, she called out, "Hello?"

Leaving everything but the cooler behind, she walked into the main part of the cabin. It was just as she remembered. The den was the heart of the house. All the other rooms extended from there. The kitchen stood to her left, an extension of the living area. The stairway to the upper bedrooms and attics was to her right, along with the hallway that led to two large bedrooms.

She had expected to find a fire burning in the den when she arrived. Rosie loved that big stone fireplace and often asked Milton to light it before summer even ended.

"Milton? Rosie?" Nicole called as she moved through the cabin. Only the echo of her own footsteps greeted her.

Where is everyone?

"Nana?"

Nicole remembered the cooler she held and headed to the kitchen. Setting it on the counter, she opened the refrigerator. Food filled each of the shelves and the door. Obviously someone had been here. And recently, too.

She crossed the kitchen to the back door. She checked the lock to see if the deadbolt was in place or if someone had left it open. It was locked. She went back to the den and looked around again. Everything appeared neat and clean. No luggage or personal effects lying around like she would expect to find with a house full of guests.

She clicked on the main lights in the den. She hadn't arrived so late that everyone would be in bed by now. Nicole headed toward the main bedrooms, turning on lights as she went.

Both of the bedroom doors were open and the light from the hallway spilled into each, allowing her to see the unoccupied beds. She couldn't even find any luggage sitting around.

What is going on?

She pulled her cell phone from her purse and dialed Nana's pre-programmed phone number.

"Hello?" Nana answered.

"Where is everyone?" Nicole asked.

"I'm here at the house. Where are you?"

"I'm at the cabin."

"What are you doing out there?" Nana asked.

"Milton and Rosie's party is tomorrow, right?"

"Oh no, honey. Did you not get my message?"

"What message?"

"The one I left on your work phone earlier."

"No-o-o-o." Nicole drew out the word. "What did it say?"

"When Milton returned from the cabin this afternoon after hearing the latest weather update, he decided he didn't want everyone going out there with the big snowstorm moving in. They're going to reschedule the party for another weekend."

Nicole groaned into the phone.

"You said you drove all the way out there?"

"Yep."

"Oh dear. Were the roads okay?" Nana asked.

"They were coming out here. But I doubt they'll stay that way much longer. The snow started sticking to the roads not long after I crossed the big bridge."

"Well, you best stay put until the morning. Or just stay for the whole weekend. You know Milton and Rosie won't mind if you do. It'd do you some good to get away from your job for a bit."

"Yeah, well, it doesn't look like I have much choice right now," she grumbled.

"You could still look for those paintings I told you about while you're there."

She had promised Bob that she'd do a report on the paintings either way. "That's true. Okay, so maybe it won't be a wasted weekend after all."

"Of course it won't be. You've needed to take some time off

22

for a while now. Why don't you do a little reading and just relax while you're there? No one will bother you all weekend."

Nicole remembered the smell of the pine and clean, crisp winter air when she'd gotten out of the car. Perhaps it would do her some good. She could clear her head and decide what she wanted to do about *Art at Dark* and whether or not she wanted to fight Yvonne for control.

"So, tell me what I'm looking for if I'm to find these long-lost paintings of yours."

Charlotte described what she could remember of the paintings and where she last saw them. From what Nicole could tell, if she found Nana's old writing chest, she'd most likely find the paintings. How hard could it be to find a chest?

When she finished talking with Nana, she located the thermostat and turned the heat up to a reasonable level. Next she scouted out the lower bedrooms in order to decide where she wanted to sleep. When she visited the cabin as a child the adults always took the lower bedrooms and she and her cousins slept upstairs on somewhat uncomfortable bunk beds and roll-aways. It would be nice to not have to sleep on those lumpy mattresses.

Something drew her to the bedroom that faced the back of the cabin. It had always been her favorite. It had a high ceiling and jutted out beyond the back of the cabin. The whole south wall had been made of glass, including the French doors that opened to the wraparound porch. Because of all the windows, it had the best view of the lake. Every morning it caught enough of the first rays of the sun to wake you without being direct or intrusive.

The curtains had been updated along with the windows since she'd last visited, but what captured her attention was the massive four-poster bed in the center of the wall. It sat high enough that children probably needed the steps at the foot of the bed frame to climb in. The dark wood of the bed contrasted against the pale wood of the walls and the floor, but the style of the carvings helped it blend in with the room. The deep-burgundy and gold bed linens had a satin finish and added a luxurious touch.

The puffy pillows scattered across the top would be easy to get lost in. It would be relaxing just to spend the night in that bed.

That decision made, she headed back to the den to retrieve her bags. Once she deposited her bags and plugged in her cell phone to recharge, she headed to the kitchen to find something to eat. She put her soda in the refrigerator but left the cereal bars and chips on the counter.

Milton and Rosie went overboard with the food. She checked her watch. It was too late to call them tonight, but she would first thing in the morning to find out which dishes they did or didn't mind her getting into.

She walked from room to room, observing the changes that had been made to the cabin over the years. Not only had the exterior windows been updated, but the appliances in the kitchen and the electronics and furniture in the living room had as well.

None of the pieces were extravagant. Everything seemed to have been selected for comfort and durability. Yet it blended together wonderfully. After living in a world where art and beauty were touted, it was nice to just *be*. To be comfortable. To be practical. To be herself. Even if it was only for a short while. Strange that it hadn't occurred to her before now how tense she'd been.

She searched for the remote to the television then flipped to the local news. As she headed back to the kitchen, she heard the reporter talking about a car accident involving a jackknifed truck on the main highway through Sumner. All four lanes were blocked and traffic had been rerouted. Nicole stopped and listened to the rest of the report. With the rapidly deteriorating weather and road conditions, the authorities doubted they would be able to get a wrecker in before morning.

"Good thing I didn't plan on driving home tonight," she mumbled.

She cut a small portion from one of the casserole dishes in the refrigerator and heated it in the microwave. Then she added lunch meat and a roll and headed to the den to curl up on the couch. As much as she longed to listen to the crackle of the wood in a roaring fire, the exertion needed to grab wood from outside and to get it going didn't seem worth it. Instead she watched the rest of the news while she ate, but found herself critiquing each of their spots.

Disgusted with herself for not being able to go one evening without thinking of work, Nicole hit the power button on the remote then took her plate to the kitchen. Standing at the sink, she became hypnotized by the falling snow outside the window. It covered the driveway now. Only tiny spots of gravel could be seen through the blanket of white. The occasional clink on the glass panes hinted at sleet mixed in with the flakes. It would be a winter wonderland when she woke in the morning.

She rinsed her plate before heading to the bedroom to dress for bed. After washing up and changing into her favorite flannel pants and faded T-shirt, she returned to the den to find a book. Rosie was a romance junkie. There were bound to be a dozen scattered around the cabin.

As she skimmed book covers a noise on the back porch caught her attention. With the blinds closed on all the windows, she couldn't be sure what the source might be. It could be a raccoon or some other harmless animal trying to find someplace warm for the night. She peeked through the blinds on the window behind the television and saw footprints in the snow on the porch.

The prints led to the back-room door. Whoever had walked across the porch was now in the back room trying to get through the door.

Nicole scurried to the fireplace and grabbed the first thing she could find that might make a suitable weapon. She gripped the handle of the fire poker and stared at the door even as she mentally kicked herself for not making sure it was still locked. Who would be out so late at night in the middle of a snowstorm?

The handle jiggled then the door swung open. A large stack of firewood came through, followed by a bundled-up yet obviously masculine snowman. When she saw his face, the adrenaline she had been building up left her body in a rush. Her knees weakened and she began to shake.

A hungry polar bear would have been preferable to Randy Stephenson.

CHAPTER SIX

"Nicki."

Nicole's pulse quickened and warmth blossomed in the base of her belly at the sound of her name on his lips. The deep, rich timbre of his voice had always gotten to her. It was like a gentle caress to her soul. No one else called her Nicki. She would never let them, since no one would ever be able to say it quite like Randy. With a wealth of feeling and sensual promises behind it.

A wave of emotion and memories threatened to overtake her. She grasped every drop of control she could muster. "What are you doing here?"

Randy smiled over the pile of wood he held. "It's good to see you, too." He took another step in and kicked the door shut behind him. "Are you planning to use that poker on me or can I go ahead and bring in this wood?"

Nicki looked at the poker in her hands. "Oh." She dropped it back into the rack and stepped away from the fireplace to give him room. Crossing her arms, she asked, "Did Milton and Rosie know you were coming?"

Randy stacked the logs in the corner near the fireplace. Even through the layers of winter clothing he wore, Nicole could see the play of muscles across Randy's back. It stirred a longing she thought she buried long ago.

"Of course." He shot a questioning look in her direction as he put the last couple of logs in place. When he finished, he stood, wiped his hands on his jeans, and looked around the den. "Is everyone in bed already?"

She gave in to the need to put some kind of barrier between her and Randy and stepped behind the closest chair. And it had

26

nothing to do with the fact that she wore comfy but not very flattering pajamas. *Liar.*

"Everyone like who?" she asked.

Randy frowned. "Pop. Gram." He shrugged. "Everyone who came for the party."

"You mean the cancelled party?"

He stopped arranging the logs and faced her. His brow was furrowed into a frown. "Pop and Gram's party got cancelled? Why didn't anyone tell me?"

Nicole mumbled, "The message they left you must have been as effective as the one I got."

"You didn't know it had been cancelled either?"

Nicole shook her head. "Not until I got here."

"Who else is here?"

"No one."

A strange look crossed Randy's face. "How do you know it's cancelled? They could still be on the way."

Nicole shook her head. "I called Nana. She said she'd left a message on my voice mail at work but I didn't get it before I left the office."

"Why did they cancel the party?"

"Milton said he didn't want anyone driving in the weather." She tipped her head toward the one uncovered window in the kitchen. "For obvious reasons."

The snowflakes were much bigger than when she arrived. And there were so many coming down it was hard to see.

Randy tucked his hands into his pants pockets and followed her gaze out the window. "The roads had a little buildup when I got off the main highway. If I hadn't passed all the emergency vehicles, I would have been here sooner. How much snow are they forecasting?"

Nicole tugged on the charm that hung from the chain around her neck. "I'm not sure. Six to ten inches, depending on where you're at."

"Man. I drove all the way down here for nothing." He shook his head then looked in her direction. "I guess there's nothing to be done about it now, though, huh?"

She considered him for a moment. "No. At least not until morning."

"Is that when you'll be heading out?"

"I don't know." Nicole hesitated. "I thought about staying for the weekend, but I can head back in the morning if you want to stay."

"You don't have to leave just because I'm here."

"It would probably be best." When Nicole saw he was going to argue with her, she held up one hand to stop him. "But we can wait and see what the roads look like in the morning."

Randy nodded in agreement then looked out the window again. "I better go get my bag before I can't find my way to the car."

"Did you park in the back?"

"Yeah. I thought there might be others coming in, so I parked near the barn." He grimaced. "Now I know why there was so much room back there. I thought Pop had parked a few cars inside the barn."

Nicole snorted in disbelief. "He wouldn't have been able to get one car in there, much less several." The last time she saw the inside of the barn it had been stacked to the ceiling with old furniture that Milton wanted to restore. *Someday.* Everyone knew he'd never get around to working on any of it. He just liked to collect the pieces and talk about what he might do with them.

Randy chuckled. "Actually, we got Pop to clean it out a few years ago when they replaced the windows and stuff. The workers needed a place to store their materials during the renovation."

Nicole's jaw slackened. "What did you do with all that furniture?"

"Each of the kids and grandkids took pieces. The rest we took to an auctioneer in Sumner." He looked at her with a quizzical expression. "You haven't been here in a while, have you?"

She shook her head. "No." Nicole took a deep breath, not willing to admit to *why* she hadn't visited in so long. She moved from behind the oversized chair she'd been all but hiding behind and sat in it. "You'd better go get your stuff before it freezes."

"Oh, yeah." Randy headed to the back-room door. "Back in a minute."

"I'll be right here," she mumbled to his retreating back. Glad for the chance to reassemble her thoughts, she stared absently out the window at the falling snow and wondered what to do now that she was face-to-face with Randy again. Over the years she imagined more than one scenario and what she would say to him if she ever had a chance. Right now every one of those ideas escaped her.

What do you say to the man who broke your heart eight years ago? Do you tell him about the baby you lost that he never knew about? *His* baby.

She'd lived through it and wondered if they weren't all better off the way things turned out. She was over Randy and telling him what she'd been through would be an emotional bloodletting she didn't want to endure. It wasn't worth it. Besides, what difference would it make after all this time?

CHAPTER SEVEN

Randy stomped the snow off his boots at the back-porch door before entering the small storage room that acted as a weather barrier to the cabin. Like so many years before, he was alone at Pops' and Grams' cabin with Nicki Cartwright. Perhaps he was being given a chance to explain why he left and why he'd never been able to face her and apologize.

When he opened the cabin door, he saw her sitting in the same place. She had curled up in the oversized chair and wrapped a blanket around herself. She seemed to be lost in her thoughts. Was she as unsettled as him to be here? Or were thoughts of someone else distracting her? A pang of jealousy caught him off guard.

That was stupid. She'd probably had several boyfriends in the last eight years. He had no claim on Nicki's affections. And it wasn't as if he had been chaste.

Still he couldn't shake the primal urge to pound on his chest and roar at any other man who might get within ten feet of Nicki. Randy shook the thought from his head and kicked the porch door closed behind him. "It's sleeting more than it is snowing now."

"I thought I heard ice hitting the window."

"The roads will be slick in the morning if this keeps up."

She nodded in agreement. "I guess you got here just in time."

Randy held her gaze. "Looks like it."

Something unspoken passed between them. Nicki squirmed in her chair. It made him want to disturb her. To get under her skin and never leave. But he didn't want her to be afraid of him. Besides, it wasn't as if he was going to bite her.

At least not in a bad way.

And, even then, only if she asked.

Nicole fingered one corner of the blanket, twisting it around and around. "So, how have you been?"

"I've been fine." He walked to the couch across from where Nicki sat and dropped his bags on the floor next to it. "Business is booming." He slipped his coat off and draped it across the back. He rested his elbows on his thighs and looked her in the eye. "You look good, Nicki," he said quietly. Honestly.

"Most people call me Nicole."

Randy smiled at her attempt to sidestep his compliment. He scanned her from head to toe, at least what he could see from beneath the blanket. "You still look like Nicki to me."

She blushed under his scrutiny. "Yeah, well…" she stammered. "What have you been up to? I heard you started your own architectural firm."

He leaned against the back of the couch and draped one arm across the top of the cushions. "I did. Actually it's a partnership with one of the guys I went to school with. We specialize in renovating historical buildings to make them commercial friendly without losing the historical value of the property."

Nicki nodded. "Didn't your firm get some kind of award recently for your work in one of the Chicago suburbs?"

"Yeah, we did." It pleased him that she kept tabs on him. "How did you know? I haven't even told Pop or Gram yet."

"It must have come across in one of the newswires at the station." A faint blush appeared on her cheeks. "Don't worry, though." She pulled one slender hand from under the blanket and waved it in the air as if to brush away the thought. "I haven't said anything to them. So, if you wanted to surprise them, it isn't ruined."

"Thanks. It's not that big of a deal even if you did tell them. I just wanted to surprise Gram. She always makes a big deal about things like that. I thought she'd get a kick out of housing the plaque for me."

"She'll love it."

In reality, the award meant a lot to him and Vince. It would open many doors for their firm and create new business opportunities. New business meant they might be able to open a second office like they had talked about for a couple of years.

"What about you? How's your television show going?"

"Good." Nicki nodded. "I get to interview local artists and keep up with new exhibits in town. So, yeah, it's good."

"Glad to hear it."

Nicki continued to nod. Was she trying to convince him that it was good? Or herself?

"Gram said the show was a new concept for the station and they went out on a limb to give you a chance with it," he prompted.

"Yeah." She smiled. Now she looked like the Nicki he remembered. "At the time, no one in the state had done anything like it. Bob took a chance on me and the show." She tilted her head to one side. "It's been working out. We've been getting great ratings and it supports the governor's campaign to promote the arts in the community."

"Do I sense a but in there?"

"Well…" Nicki's voice trailed off as she turned her head away. "We'll see how it turns out."

"What's the problem? Don't you *like* doing the show?"

When she faced him he saw a troubled look in her eye before she could mask it.

"Mostly. I love doing the interviews and the research and going to the gallery openings. The politics that go with running a show get old after a while but it is part of the deal."

Once again he was unsure who she needed to convince. Before he could press her, she changed the subject.

"So, how long were you planning to stay around?"

Was she already trying to get rid of him? "I didn't make definite return plans. Through the weekend at least."

Randy surprised himself with his answer. He'd told Vince he'd be back Sunday night, but something about Nicki's prickly attitude made him want to stay just to get to the bottom of it. "What about you? Did you take vacation days to come out here?"

"A couple, but I can head back in the morning."

"Seriously. Don't leave because of me."

"I don't think it's a good idea for me to stay." Nicki pulled the blanket up to cover her arms and chest.

"Why? We're two grown adults."

"Two adults who have a history."

Randy couldn't resist asking, "Did I ruin things between us so badly that you can't even stand to be in the same place as me?"

Nicki held his gaze before answering. "I'd like to think not. But

I spent so many years putting it behind me that I'm not sure I want to go back into that dark place to figure it out."

Randy nodded, more in acknowledgement that he'd heard what she said than agreement. "For what it's worth, I'm sorry."

"What exactly are you apologizing for?"

"For walking away and not telling you why. For not returning your calls. For not getting in touch with you even once over the last eight years." In a softer tone he added, "For hurting you."

Nicki nodded stiffly and turned her face away.

Randy's heart twisted painfully in his chest. He'd hurt her and he regretted it more than anything he'd ever done. What could he do to make it right?

He crossed his arms over his chest and stared into the empty fireplace. Memories of the day he'd left Sumner for Chicago flitted through his mind.

Nicki stood from the chair, halting his trip down memory lane.

"I think I'll turn in. Are you going to stay up for a while?" she asked.

"Probably only long enough to grab a bite to eat. I'm a little tired from the drive."

"I took a casserole out of the freezer when I got here. It's in the fridge. There's some lunch meat, too."

"That'll work. Thanks."

Nicki turned to go then stopped. "I, uh, I took the back bedroom. It looked like both of the bedrooms were made up down here. I didn't check upstairs, though."

"I'm pretty sure the drive will catch up with me pretty soon and I won't care where I crash. I'll just take the other one down here."

"Okay. Well, goodnight then."

Randy watched until Nicki disappeared around the corner. Even in the loose-fitting pajamas and T-shirt, he could tell she worked to stayed in shape. She had always been delicate looking but now she had womanly curves in all the right places. His body hardened just thinking about exploring those curves.

It may be too late for regrets but perhaps it wasn't too late to begin something new.

CHAPTER EIGHT

Nicole closed the bedroom door and slumped against it. She looked at the massive bed in front of her without actually seeing it.

God. Randy.

She never expected to see him again. Part of her had hoped that she wouldn't.

He was even better looking than she remembered. His hair had turned a darker shade of blond than it used to be and he styled it in a neat, masculine cut. When he'd taken off his coat in the living room she thought she might swallow her tongue. It was apparent Randy didn't just sit at a desk all day. From the width and shape of his shoulders and arms, he had to work out or do some kind of physical activity on a regular basis.

Definitely drool worthy.

Her stomach flip-flopped at the thought of getting close enough to drool on Randy. No matter how worthy of it he might be, that would be heartbreak waiting to happen.

She'd barely survived the last one. She didn't need another. Especially with everything she had going on at work right now.

Keeping Yvonne's fuchsia-tipped paws off *Art at Dark* would require all of her brain cells. Assuming she really wanted to go in that direction. And if she decided to keep *Art at Dark*, she should also answer the question of why. Would she be keeping it because it was a career path she wanted to follow or a primal need to keep Yvonne from taking it over and ruining it?

Nicole rubbed one hand across her face to wipe away the strain her thoughts were causing. She headed to the adjoining bathroom to finish getting ready for bed. When she returned to the bedroom, the four-poster bed distracted her. She pulled back the thick comforter and sheet then climbed up onto the bed. Her knees sank into the mattress. It felt as if she were sitting on top of a cloud.

Too bad she and Randy had a history. This weekend might have been a great opportunity to jump-start her dormant libido. The bed made a perfect backdrop for sensual encounters.

Randy had been a good-looking guy but he was a panty-dropping man. Her traitorous body had already made up its mind about him. Or, more specifically, what it would like to do to and with him. Never mind what he had done to her heart years ago.

Would it kill her to have a quick fling with him before she left? Maybe she could even be the one to love and leave 'em.

He would probably only be around for a day or two before returning to Chicago, which meant no long-term commitment. But *Art at Dark* kept her far too busy for any kind of serious relationship. She also didn't have to worry about him being a starstruck fan, or worse, a potential stalker. He was a longtime friend of the family. He didn't live in Springfield and didn't watch her show.

She shuddered as she recalled a couple of run-ins she'd had with overzealous fans. Luckily she'd been out with friends and they were able to fend them off with a little help from security. It had still been scary. It wasn't as if she were some big movie star, just a local reporter with a special segment a couple times each week.

She couldn't imagine what true celebrities went through. They were probably hounded not only by rabid fans but also the press. Having their trash dug through. Reporters sticking cameras in their faces everywhere they went. That life held no appeal for her.

Why am I sitting here justifying the reasons I should sleep with him? That is the way to madness.

She turned around and punched the pillows behind her then flopped against them. As far she knew, he could be seeing someone. Or even engaged.

Her heart twisted. What if he did have a fiancée? He'd had more than enough time to meet someone and get involved. It was highly unlikely that he'd been celibate all these years. She snorted to herself. He was a guy. Of course there had been other women over the years.

Even she had been involved in a couple of semi-serious relationships but things never meshed. She often wondered if it had been due to the fact that no one had ever made her feel the way she had with Randy.

There had never been the level of passion or even comfort with anyone else. She'd thought about giving in once, but something deep inside her just couldn't settle. If she ever did marry, she wanted it to be for good. The only way a relationship could last was if both parties were open and honest. That included about how they felt about each other down to the bone.

She sighed.

When she realized she was just staring off into space dwelling on things that were better left alone, she slipped out of the bed and sauntered to the window on the far side of the room. She turned the lever on the blinds so she could look outside. The snow continued to steadily fall. From what accumulated on the rail of the back porch, there were probably a couple of inches on the ground.

That would make for nasty driving conditions tomorrow.

The snowplows should be working on the roads first thing in the morning, though. Despite wanting to look for the paintings Nana told her about, it would be best if she returned to Springfield as soon as possible.

Nicole closed the blinds again. As much as she'd love to lie in that big bed and watch the snow fall, the blinds blocked out a little of the cold coming through the windows. She turned the overhead light off then crawled back under the comforter.

Her last thought as she sank into the pile of pillows was that her thick, fuzzy socks would help keep her feet warm through the night, but it would have been nicer to curl up against a big, warm body. Especially one with blond hair and blue eyes. It made her ache in more than one way.

CHAPTER NINE

"Randy…"

Nicki whispered in her sleep, making Randy's cock harden in response. He ached to slip under the covers and feel her body curled against him.

"Nicki, honey, you need to wake up." He made a fist to stop himself from touching her.

Nicole turned onto her side, facing him. One hand reached out as if seeking his warmth. She mumbled something in her sleep that he didn't understand.

Randy gave in to the temptation to lean over and push the hair back that had fallen across the side of her face. He stroked her cheek with his thumb, allowing himself the luxury of drinking in the sight of her relaxed and at peace.

Her eyes slowly opened. He held her gaze, letting the warmth seep into his soul. With one unguarded look, he knew there was a chance she still cared for him. Unfortunately the moment didn't last long. Nicki sat up in the bed and pulled the blanket around her like a shield.

"What are you doing?"

"The power went off and I thought it might get too cold in here for you."

She looked around the room. A little light crept in around the blinds on the windows but, given the amount of cloud cover, not much. The lantern Randy had brought with him illuminated the doorway behind them.

Falling sleet pinged against some of the windows, hinting at the reason for the power outage.

"Oh," she said as she pushed a lock of hair behind one ear.

"I built a fire in the den. I thought you might be more comfortable sleeping on one of the couches."

"How long has it been off?"

"Probably two or three hours." He looked down at his watch. "It's about four now."

Nicole wrapped her arms around herself and shivered. Randy wanted to pull her onto his lap and chase the cold away.

Instead he moved toward the door. "If you're okay in here, I'll let you get back to sleep. I thought I'd bunk on the couch and make sure the fire stays lit so the cabin doesn't get too cold."

"Good idea. I'll come in there after I change into something warmer."

Randy nodded. "Okay." Before he slipped out the door, he took one last look at Nicki. Seeing her sitting in the middle of that bed with her hair tumbling around her shoulders tugged at him. Memories flashed though his mind. Some were of Nicki emerging from the water with her hair slicked back, droplets running down her back. Others were of her sitting on the back porch in the morning sunshine as she brushed the tangles out of her long hair. The ones that hit home were of her leaning over him, her hair tickling his chest as she rode them both to fulfillment.

Nicki looked in his direction but he stayed in the shadows to make sure she didn't know where his thoughts had been.

He left the lantern on the dresser and pulled the door closed behind him. Returning to the den before he said or did something stupid would be the best course of action.

Once in the den he restacked the firewood to distract himself. Good thing he brought a couple of armfuls from the woodpile to the back porch last night before he came inside. They should have enough to make it through the day without hiking down the hill for more.

Of course, if I can't stop thinking about getting Nicki naked, chopping wood might be just the thing to relieve some of this sexual frustration.

He hadn't seen her for more than eight years except in pictures or on television. During that time there had been no shortage of women. Yet none of them affected him the way Nicki had.

It took most of the last eight years to realize that every woman he dated or even just slept with, he compared to Nicki. None of them had measured up to her or to what they'd had together. When that realization hit, he knew how wrong he had been to leave her. He knew he had to apologize. If nothing else, he needed to know if what they'd shared had been as strong and true as he remembered. Or had time made it seem bigger and better than it really had been?

Given his reaction to Nicki so far, he'd bet the former.

"Wow. I didn't realize how cold it had gotten back there until I came in here."

The sound of Nicki's voice jerked Randy out of his thoughts. She stood just inside the den wearing a pair of baggy sweatpants and a sweatshirt. Knowing how cold natured she used to be, he'd bet she had more clothes beneath those. She grabbed a blanket from the nearby chair and wrapped it around her shoulders. Despite all the layers she wore, Randy wanted nothing more than to get his hands on her.

He cleared his throat. "It doesn't take long when the temp outside is around the freezing mark."

Nicki went to the foyer and looked out the window next to the front door. Her voice echoed across the wooden floor into the den. "It's completely covered out there."

She lingered at the window, making him wonder if she was hesitant to be near him.

"And there's ice over the snow, isn't there?" she asked.

"I'm afraid so." He wanted to comfort her and ease the worry in her voice but doubted it would be well received. "We'll be fine. We have enough wood to keep us at least somewhat comfortable until the power comes back on."

"But that means the roads are going to be really nasty."

Randy followed her to the foyer, deliberately trapping her in the confined area. The thought of her venturing out onto those roads sent a bigger chill down his spine than the cold air. "Nicki, it would be madness for you to try to drive home in this weather even if the roads *are* open."

Her eyes widened. He wondered if it was due to his proximity or the fact that he'd all but growled at her.

She took a step back. "But I can't stay here with you."

"Why not?"

"Because," she sputtered. Pulling the blanket tighter, she put more distance between them. "I just can't."

"Nicki, what are you afraid of?" He reached for her.

"I'm not afraid of anything. I just—" She sidestepped him and moved into the dining room adjacent to the foyer. "I just don't think it's a great idea to stay. You're—" She pressed her lips together.

"I'm what?"

"Nothing." She scampered into the kitchen through the doorway at the other end of the room.

Randy took a deep breath, prayed for patience, then followed her into the kitchen. Nicki pulled a coffee mug out of one of the cabinets as he entered. She didn't even look his way. She just added water to the lifeless coffeemaker sitting on the counter.

Somewhat amused by her obvious distraction, he asked, "What are you planning to do with that?"

"Make coffee." Awareness that without power, no coffee would be dripping out anytime soon swept over her expression. "Oh. Well, crap." She dropped the spoon on the counter with a thud. "I have to go without coffee? Can this day get any worse?"

Randy did his best to not laugh at her frustration. "I planned to heat some water in the fireplace in a bit so, no, you won't have to go without coffee." He reached into the cabinet next to the stove and took out one of the metal pots that looked sturdy enough to withstand the open flame. "You don't have it all that bad out here. I'll be able to keep us reasonably warm. We have food and water. And we have the added bonus of no distractions from the outside world."

If possible, she frowned even more. Pulling the blanket tighter around her, she tucked the edge under her arms then hugged her middle. "But it's just you and me out here," she mumbled.

Randy held her gaze and reminded her, "It's been just you and me out here before, Nicki."

Even with the low lighting he could see her cheeks had turned a delightful shade of pink.

"Yes, well, back then I was young and foolish enough to think that you loved me. I'm not so young and I'm definitely not that foolish anymore."

Randy caught the glitter of tears in her eyes before she turned away.

God.

Her anger he could take. But her tears cut him right to the core. If she had stabbed him with a knife it would have been less painful.

CHAPTER TEN

I need to get out of here. But the roads suck. Even if I could get my car up the drive and onto the main highway, is it worth the risk of ending up in a ditch? Or worse?

Maybe.

Dammit. Of all the people on the planet, why did he have to be here?

Nicole paced the length of the den as she railed at herself. Then it occurred to her that she was yelling at herself in her head. A short of laughter escaped. Maybe getting trapped up here with Randy had been the last straw and her sanity finally took off at a run.

She flopped into the oversized chair closest to the fire, pulled her knees up so her feet were tucked under her, and made a cocoon with the blanket she had been clinging to like a lifeline.

True to his word, Randy managed to heat a pot of water in the fireplace.

Despite the emotional upheaval of seeing him again, it was nice to have someone here with her. She would have been able to manage without heat or electricity *somehow*, but she was grateful she didn't have to fumble around in the dark trying to figure it out on her own.

If she were going to be stuck at the cabin for a while, she might as well start looking for the paintings Nana had told her about. Finding out what her great-grandmother brought back from France held a lot of appeal. But why would they have been tucked away instead of hung on the walls somewhere? Hopefully the paintings weren't created by one of those abstract artists and required deep thought and introspection to understand what they meant to show.

As much as she loved art, abstracts had never appealed to her.

She would rather appreciate a piece for the artist's ability to capture the moment, the emotion, and the variety of colors. Finding little details like the reflection of the morning light on a drop of dew falling from the end of a leaf enticed her far more than a debate of what the dewdrop represented.

Searching the attics would give her something to focus on instead of her lingering attraction to Randy. In the still of the early morning hours she had difficulty overlooking his presence. Damn him.

Otherwise, the peace and quiet would be relaxing. No television or radio. No air blowing through the vents from the heater. Not even the gentle hum of appliances running in the background. Just the sizzle and pop of the fire and the rush of the wind trying to force its way into the cabin.

A loud crack followed by a crash just outside the cabin made both of them jump.

"What was that?" Nicole exclaimed as she struggled to get out of her warm cocoon so she could follow Randy to the kitchen.

He leaned over the sink and looked out the window. "Sounded like a tree coming down."

"Good God," Nicole muttered as she strained to look out the same window without brushing against him. "I hope it didn't hit anything."

Unable to see what had caused the noise, she and Randy moved to the dining room, which looked out on to the front porch.

"Oh, man," Randy muttered after opening the blinds on the large picture window.

"My car!" Nicole pressed closer to the glass, trying to get a better look.

There was just enough light to see the tree lying across the gravel drive in front of the cabin, right next to where Nicole had parked. The front of her car had been covered by limbs, making it difficult to see how much damage it might have. It looked as if the largest part of the tree missed her car but there were bound to be scratches on the hood at the very least.

"I just paid if off," she whimpered.

"Dang. I'm sorry, Nicki. It might not have hurt anything major," Randy offered in the way of comfort.

"But... My car..."

Randy put one arm around her and gave her a quick hug before turning away from the window. "I need to check the outside of the cabin to make sure the tree didn't pull any electric lines down when it fell."

Nicole remained rooted at the window, stunned not only by the sight outside but also by the solid feel of Randy during his all too brief show of concern. Part of her yearned to be as close and as intimate as they had been years before. An even bigger part of her shrank in terror at the possibility of the heartache that would lead to.

The sound of Randy zipping up his coat in the foyer broke her out of her thoughts. He winked as he pulled on his gloves. "Don't laugh if I fall on my ass out there."

Before she could think of a response, the front door closed behind him. She turned and watched from the window. He descended the porch steps with care and shuffled toward the drive then turned and looked up at the cabin roofline. There must not have been anything to be concerned about, for it didn't take long before he continued toward her car.

She chewed on her thumbnail and debated going outside. Had the tree hurt her little car? And if it had, how would she get home? She couldn't ask Randy to drive her all the way to Springfield. And there was no way she'd risk Nana getting out on these roads.

Maybe she should go out and look. But she'd need to find her boots first, and right now she couldn't remember where she had left them. Perhaps it would be best if she remained inside. After all, there was no point in *both* of them getting cold.

It wasn't because she wanted to avoid being around him.

Nicole rolled her eyes at her own foolishness.

Randy squatted near the front and looked under the branches. He stood then maneuvered around the limbs scattered across the snow. She couldn't see much as he inspected the rest of the tree and the area around it. He shook his head a couple of times. Hopefully that didn't mean bad news.

When he walked to the back of the cabin she lost sight of him.

Giving up her station at the window, she returned to the living room. She grabbed the oven mitts Randy had left on the mantle, took the pot of water out of the fire, and set it on the stone ledge. Then she added another log to the fire to build it up again. Randy would need to get warm when he came back in.

She headed to the kitchen to grab coffee mugs and the supplies she'd need for hot chocolate. When she heard Randy stomping around on the back porch, she unlocked the door so he could get in.

Based on the back-and-forth footsteps, she guessed Randy added logs to the stash on the back porch from the outside pile. At least he wouldn't have to add one to the fire now.

A gust of chilled air blew in when he came through the back door with an armful of wood.

"Everything okay out there?" she asked as he set the logs near the fireplace.

"I think so, but won't know for sure until the sun comes up." He turned and shrugged off his coat. "At least I didn't see any electricity arcing from the power lines or out of the house."

"Well, thank God for that," she muttered. Then almost reluctantly she asked, "What about my car? Did it get squished?"

"Actually, no." Randy sighed as he dropped onto the end of the sofa. He unlaced his boots and added, "But I wouldn't plan on going anywhere anytime soon if I were you."

"Why not?" She grimaced, afraid of the answer.

"The tree is blocking most of the drive. The circle drive is completely blocked." He ran one hand through his hair after taking his stocking cap off. "It's going to take some effort to cut that tree up and drag it out of the way. And that's after we clear off enough ice so I can work without slipping and falling with the axe or chain saw in my hand."

Nicole shook off the horrible image of Randy getting hurt and took a deep breath. She might as well get used to the idea of spending a few days locked away with him. Neither of them could do much about it right now anyway.

The Pollyanna part of her wondered if perhaps there was a reason they were here. Maybe she needed to resolve the hurt she'd carried all these years so she could move past it.

Who knew?

She retrieved the mugs, filled them with hot water, and mixed in the chocolate then handed one to Randy. "Here. This will warm you up without the caffeine kick of coffee so you can get some more sleep." She smiled at him. "You look like you didn't get much last night."

He took her offering. "Thanks." He held her gaze as he took a sip. "I promised you coffee, though."

"That's okay. You can make it later when you cook breakfast."

He snorted into his mug. "Me? Cook breakfast?"

"You know I won't be able to whip up much more than cereal under these conditions."

He smiled and nodded. "Probably true if you haven't been camping in a while."

"Nope." She returned his smile as she flopped into the chair she had been sitting in earlier. Pointing to her chest with her thumb, she told him with pride, "Been a city girl for some time now."

"What makes you think I've had any experience cooking over an open fire lately?"

"Guys never forget stuff like that," she said with certainty.

He grunted. "We'll see."

It occurred to her they had slipped into the familiar teasing they used to exchange. It was nice in a way. But would it last? Would she ever be at ease around him again or would the past keep creeping up and getting in the way of them even being friends?

Did she want to just be friends with him?

Something cried out from depths of her soul that she was ten kinds of a fool for even considering it.

CHAPTER ELEVEN

Randy let himself relax enough to doze while they waited for the morning light. When he'd heard the ice pinging on the roof and the nearby tree branches he had silently thanked God. The fallen tree had been a blessing. Not that he wanted Nicki's car smashed. But between the slick roads and the blocked drive, she would be stuck here for at least one more day. Two or three, if he were lucky.

He could tell from the panicked look on Nicki's face when she realized the roads were iced over, she didn't want to be trapped here alone with him. He had his work cut out for him if he wanted to make it up to her for walking away.

Walking? There had been no walking. Hell, he'd run. All the way to Chicago.

Sure his mother had needed him, but it had also been an excuse to go. He'd been young, unsure of his future, and felt trapped. But just because he'd been lost and struggled with learning things about himself and what he wanted to do with his life, that didn't excuse his behavior. He should have told her what he had been feeling. Instead he had been a coward and hurt her more by just shutting her out.

After he moved to Chicago, Gram Rosie made it her business to keep him updated on the highlights of Nicki's life and her general well-being. He didn't know how much Gram, Pop, or Nicki's grandmother knew about their relationship, but everyone knew they had been close at one time. That's why he struggled to believe it had only been coincidence neither he nor Nicki received word about the cancelled party.

Despite Nicki's attempts to put on a brave front, he could tell she still had feelings for him. As long as she felt *something* for him, he had a chance to work his way back into her good graces. He just needed to decide how far he would be willing to go to earn her trust.

If he was going to win back her love, he would need her forgiveness, too. And now that he knew what he wanted—what he needed—he wouldn't give up without a fight.

Nicki stirred then resettled in the chair across from him. He watched her through half-raised eyelids and reminded himself why he needed to keep his distance. More than one night had been spent on the floor of this very room, with her warm, naked body wrapped over and around him. His body was anxious to relive some of those memories.

Needing a distraction before his thoughts created more of a problem than the need to adjust the blanket over his lap, he went looking for coffee and filters. He put another pot of water over the fire then worked out how to soak the grounds and filter them out again.

As soon as the grounds hit the boiling water, Nicki woke. "Is that going to be coffee?" she asked in a sleepy voice.

"I hope so."

"You're my hero," she mumbled, then stretched her arms above her head.

If only it were that easy. "So," Randy said with forced enthusiasm. "What do you want to do today? Chess? Monopoly?" Just to push it he added, "Strip poker?"

Nicki held his gaze before responding, as if she were trying to decide how serious he had been.

"Actually," she drew out the word, "I need to look for an old writing chest that Nana told me about."

He blinked in question. He'd expected her to say she wanted to clear the fallen tree off the drive immediately so she could leave. "A writing chest?"

She nodded. "The chest originally belonged to Nana's mother. She said she left it in one of the attics years ago so it wouldn't get lost or damaged during one their moves. Then she never came back to get it."

He remembered overhearing Rosie and Charlotte talking about the different places Charlotte and her husband had lived when they were first married. It seemed as if some of Charlotte's things were stored in the barn. But at this point he wouldn't know which items belonged to whom. "Did she say what the chest looked like or how big it was?"

"Nana said she thought it was about this wide," she demonstrated the width with her hands, "and this tall." She did the same to show the height. "She thought it had three drawers down the front and a hinged top."

"What color?"

"It's wood but I don't know what kind."

Randy searched his memory, trying to remember if he had ever seen anything like that in the junk cluttering the three attic spaces.

"I doubt there's more than one writing chest around here, so it can't be that hard to find," she suggested.

He shrugged. "I don't know. If it's a chest like those I've seen at auction, it will be small enough that it could be sitting out somewhere or stashed away in a closet or a larger chest. I don't remember ever seeing one."

Keeping the blanket wrapped tightly around her legs and middle, Nicki got up and penguin walked over to the fireplace. She leaned over and inhaled deeply of the coffee soaking on the fireplace ledge. When she turned to face him she had a hopeful grin on her face. "Do you think it's ready yet?"

Her childlike eagerness captivated him. "Depends on how strong you like your coffee."

"At this point I might just settle for it smelling like coffee. We can work on quality later."

He chuckled as he grabbed the pot and took it to the kitchen. Nicki followed on his heels like an anxious puppy. Once he got some of the pseudo-coffee poured into a mug, he handed it to her to taste.

"Eh." She gave the so-so sign with her hand. "But it will do." She held out her mug, silently asking for more.

"Say please."

"Please don't make me smash something heavy over your head for withholding caffeine and warmth from an addict." She gave him a sticky-sweet smile and pushed the mug in his direction.

Randy shook his head but filled the mug almost to the brim.

She blew across the top of the steaming brew then took a sip. She sighed with contentment and smiled gratefully at him. Her genuine expression made his heart turn over in his chest.

Nicki had always gotten along with everyone. She was never

demanding or pushy and usually easy to please. Little things always mattered most to her. Things like a wildflower picked from a nearby field. A quiet evening spent on the porch. A gentle kiss when she least expected it.

The urge to give in to the temptation and kiss her rode him hard.

"Nicki, I—" Randy stopped himself before he either embarrassed himself or made her panic again. She had just started to relax around him and he didn't want to risk making her run, either physically or mentally. There were a few barriers he would have to break through before she would let him get close again.

Nicki looked at him expectantly, waiting for him to continue.

"I, uh…" To give himself time to come up with a response, he poured some of the brown liquid into his own mug and placed the pot on the stovetop. "I was trying to think of how many oil lamps we had around here that could be taken up to the attic."

"Oh." She almost looked disappointed but quickly recovered. "Yeah, that's a good idea."

Randy grabbed on to the thought like a lifeline. "It may be a little cold up there even with the heat rising from the den. But if we wear our coats and lightweight gloves it will be fine in short bursts. We'll just need to make sure we don't let in too much of the cold air and make the lower floor cooler."

Nicki nodded her understanding. "Gotcha." She tilted her head to one side, a gesture he remembered well. He also remembered wanting to nibble on the part of her neck that became exposed whenever she did it.

Lost in thoughts of nibbling on Nicki, he didn't hear what she'd said. "What?"

"I said you don't have to look for the chest. I can do it."

"I don't mind." He smiled sheepishly. "Besides, it'll give me an excuse to not go outside and work on that tree."

She grimaced. "I suppose we do need to start cutting it up, don't we?"

Randy nodded. "Yes, but I'm in no hurry to work my ass off in the freezing cold only to come in to a lukewarm cabin. I'd rather wait to see if the power comes back on later today."

"That's a good point."

Randy breathed a sigh of relief.

By unspoken agreement, they migrated back to the den to sit

near the fire again.

"I will need to get my car out from underneath it soon," Nicole continued. "I didn't plan to take any more days off from work."

"If the roads are bad, I'm sure your boss will understand."

"He would, but it's not him I'm worried about."

He frowned. "Who else would give you a hard time about being gone?"

"It's just office politics." Her expression hinted there was more to it.

"Somebody after your job?" Randy leaned forward, resting his elbows on his knees.

She clutched her coffee mug with both hands and pulled her feet up into her chair again. "Well, sorta."

Randy waited for her to continue.

"Okay, it's like this." She sat up in her chair and crossed her legs so her feet were tucked under her. "I do a spot each week called *Art at Dark*. It's a show that focuses on local artists in the community. We do interviews, artist spotlights, and advertise or review any gallery openings or exhibits. It's a new concept in that it doesn't fall under the entertainment spot."

Without telling her he already knew about the show, Randy nodded his understanding. "Go on."

"The woman who controls the entertainment spot thinks *Art at Dark* should be part of her section." She rolled her eyes. "Especially since I used to work for her."

"Ah." Most likely the entire concept had come from Nicki. She had the education and the passion to make something like that come to life. He also guessed it irritated this other woman that one of her underlings had earned the spotlight.

"Ever since *Art* started getting good ratings, she's been pushing Bob to give her control of the spot. It's gotten worse in the last couple of months."

"Bob's your boss?"

"Yes."

"So if this woman has half a chance you think she'll rip your show out from underneath you?"

"In a second. That's one of the reasons I want to find this chest for Nana."

The sudden change of topic confused him. "What does the chest have to do with your show?"

Nicki smiled then leaned forward and whispered dramatically, "Nana said there may be lost treasure in there."

CHAPTER TWELVE

"Are you serious about old paintings being in this chest?" Randy asked for the fifth time as they carried oil lamps up to the attic farthest from the main staircase. They agreed to start there to minimize how much cold air crept into the main part of the cabin.

Nicole smiled. "Yes. I'm quite serious." Once she stepped into the attic, her breath turned into little puffs of condensation. She shifted a couple of boxes around on a desk in one corner so she could set the lamp down. Randy found a suitable space in the opposite corner for his.

She rubbed her gloved hands together trying to warm the cold seeping through the knit. "Nana told me she and Grandpa lived in several different places about the time her mother died. The paintings are small and could have been easily damaged or lost, so she stored them in her writing chest and left it here with Rosie and Milton."

"That had to be fifty years ago."

Nicole stopped looking over the boxes piled next to the desk and did some fast math on the time frame. "Yeah, it probably was."

Behind her, Randy searched through a similar pile of boxes and crates.

She allowed herself a moment to enjoy the view. He had changed into jeans and a heavy sweater and probably wore at least one shirt under the sweater, but even with that padding he was...well...stimulating to watch. His movements were fluid and he exuded confidence. She didn't know what the boxes he sifted through held but he moved them around like they weighed nothing.

When she realized she was staring she jerked herself back to her task before he caught her ogling him and got the wrong idea. Whatever the *wrong* idea might be, in his opinion. Either way, she didn't want to be caught gawking. She had hoped he would stay downstairs while she looked for the chest, but the thought of hidden treasure must have sparked his inner child, too, because he insisted on helping.

He had even brushed aside her idea to take one attic each, saying it would allow more cold air into the cabin if they left two doors open at the same time. Meanwhile his proximity was closer than she was comfortable with due to the size of the attic space. To make it worse, he didn't seem to share her distress at being around each other again.

The best thing she could do was act casual. As if nothing were wrong. As if her heart hadn't been broken and pieced back together. If he could pretend like the past hadn't happened, so could she.

"So, what's it like living and working in a big town like Chicago?" she asked.

"It's not all it's cracked up to be, actually."

"Why's that?"

"Oh, you know the usual complaints. Traffic, pollution, crime. The general rushing here and there, and no one seems to want to slow down. It's like most people up there thrive on it."

Surprised by his comment, she looked up from her searching. "But you don't?" Hadn't he rushed to Chicago to be in the middle of all the excitement a big city provides?

"At one time the distraction of city life was what I thought I needed." He looked over his shoulder at her. "But not anymore."

Their eyes met and held. She saw the sincerity on his face and heard it in his voice.

A heavy silence descended as they each went through box after box. Desperate to change the direction of her thoughts, she latched on to the first thing she could. "I, uh... I know it is late coming, but I'm sorry about your mom."

Randy kept digging. "Thanks. I'm just glad she didn't suffer long."

"Milton said the cancer was in her liver. When did she find out about it?"

The sound of Randy shuffling boxes stopped. "The last

summer I spent here," he said in low voice.

It took a moment for what he said to register. When it did, Nicole's heart started pounding in her chest. *Had that been the reason he left so suddenly?* Almost afraid of what she might see, she looked up and found him watching her intently.

"I told Pop not to tell anyone." Randy turned away from her and ran his hand through his hair.

"But why? Did you think we wouldn't want to help?"

"No." He faced her. "I didn't want you or anyone else to know about her drinking."

"Her drinking?" The few times his mom had visited with Randy, she didn't remember seeing her take so much as a sip.

Randy nodded. "Mom had a drinking problem. Had one for years. That's why I started coming to stay with Pop and Gram every summer." Randy shuffled a couple of boxes around. "They did what they could for Mom. Tried to get counseling for her more than once. But you just can't help someone who doesn't want to be helped."

"And that's what made her liver fail?"

"Yes and no. Her doctors said the cancer started somewhere else but since the liver had been weakened, it spread."

"I'm sorry." Nicole stepped closer and touched his arm. When he looked at her she continued, "And I'm sorry you felt like you had to go through that alone."

Randy smiled a little. "Actually, because of Mom's illness, I reconciled with my dad."

She frowned. "I thought he was some Richie Rich who took off when you were a baby."

"He did. He paid Mom child support payments every month like clockwork but he never came around. When Mom got bad I knew I'd have to take care of her and I knew I'd need money. I looked him up and asked him for a job."

Nicole blinked. How did she not know any of this? Why didn't Milton or Rosie or Nana tell her what he had gone through? They knew she cared about him. Didn't they? Lost in her own thoughts, it barely registered with her that Randy had continued his story.

"I knew he owned a big marketing firm in Chicago, so I had no trouble finding him."

As Randy went on, they dug through more boxes. Her pace became slower and less thorough since more of her mind focused on Randy's story.

"I don't remember what I thought I'd do when I found him, but he was nothing like I expected. We met, got to know each other, and I caught him up on my life. Found out he regretted not trying to make it work with Mom. In his own words, he had been a selfish rich kid who got scared of commitment and responsibility, and ran." When he looked up, some of the lingering hurt reflected in his eyes. "He even admitted it had been easier to just write a check each month then forget about it again."

Nicole's heart cried for the little boy's pain. How she could still feel so much for him amazed her. "So did he give you a job?"

"He did a lot more than that."

Randy told how his father, Howard Stephenson III, helped get him a job at a friend's company so neither of them would have to worry about issues with preferential treatment. Randy wanted to succeed because of his own hard work, not because of who his father was. He did take his father's advice and went back to school to finish his degree. Now he was a partner in one of the fastest-growing architectural firms in Chicago. And from what Nana had told her, he was doing very well.

"Once Howard and I were comfortable with each other, he starting coming around to visit Mom and me in the evenings. He even made arrangements for in-home nursing care when she needed around-the-clock care."

"Did he never marry?" Nicole asked.

"Yes, a few years after I was born he did. He said it didn't work out, though. They were only together for a couple of years before the divorce."

"What about your mom? What did she think of him reappearing in your lives?"

Randy shrugged. "I'm not completely sure. By then she needed a lot of pain medicine just to get by, so she was in and out of lucidity. Some days were better than others. She seemed glad that he had stepped in to help when I needed it and that I didn't have to do everything on my own. I think she and Howard talked through their regrets. In the end, they both seemed at peace with how things turned out."

Tears pooled in her eyes. It was sad that both Randy and his parents missed an opportunity to be a family. She turned away so he wouldn't think she pitied him.

Looking around the small space, she realized they had been through most of the stuff piled in that attic but still hadn't found the chest.

"Let's take a break," Randy suggested. "I could use some coffee."

"You go ahead. I'll clean up some of this mess then come down." Nicole kept herself busy so she wouldn't have to look at Randy even though she could feel his eyes on her. Her emotions were all mixed up and she needed some distance for a moment.

"You want me to bring you a cup?"

"Sure. That would be great." She pasted a weak smile on her face and glanced up at him. "Thanks."

When she heard the sound of his footsteps on the wooden stairs she sank to the floor.

Hearing what he went through with his mom made her heart soften toward him, and she just couldn't afford that right now. She needed to be strong and hang on to her hurt and anger to keep from being vulnerable again. She pulled her knees to her chest and rested her forehead on them.

Every part of her was still very attracted to him. She couldn't stop herself from looking in his direction every time he lifted a box just so she could see the muscles ripple under his shirt.

Even his cologne tantalized her. It smelled a little like the one he used years ago. She used to hate to wash his scent off after they had made love. Remembering the way his body felt against hers, how they fit together, and how he knew just where to touch her sent waves of warmth through her body.

She mentally shook herself to stop that line of thought. But her body still tingled.

Time had done nothing to diminish her physical reaction to him. The few times she'd had sex with anyone else only satisfied a small part of her. Something had been missing. Something she'd only ever felt with Randy.

What she wouldn't give to feel that again. Just once more.

As tempted as she was to crawl into bed with him, she could never set foot on that path without wanting more. Without her heart getting in the way.

Randy still seemed to be attracted to her. She'd caught him looking at her with a certain gleam in his eye more than once. She recognized that look. It used to mean she had turned him on by wearing a pretty dress or that she had done something he thought sexy. At least she still affected him in some small way.

Could she prove to herself, and to him, that she had moved past the hurt? Maybe her heart confused her first sexual experiences with love. Maybe now that she had experienced a little more of the world, it could be just sex. If it were then maybe she would stop comparing every man she got involved with to him. And maybe she could walk away, just like he had, without looking back.

Yeah. She could do that.

Can't I?

CHAPTER THIRTEEN

"A penny for your thoughts."

Her blush warmed her from head to toe. A vault full of cash wouldn't be enough for her to tell him what she had been thinking. No way. She stammered as she tried to come up with a response. "I was just, uh, trying to decide where to look next."

She risked a glance at Randy. He leaned against the door frame and sipped his coffee. The look on his face suggested he knew she had lied.

Deciding it would be best to work someplace else, she hopped up and grabbed the lamp. "I think I'll check the other attic while you finish up in here."

Randy didn't move as she tried to brush past him.

"You want this?"

She shivered at both the sound of his voice and the double meaning in his question. She juggled the lamp in one hand so she could take the mug he offered. Despite her brave thoughts just moments before, she knew she couldn't take that kind of risk. Instead she avoided accepting or declining any offer he made, either real or imagined. "Thanks."

She took a sip. Damn. Hot chocolate with little marshmallows. One of her favorite cold-weather treats. He'd remembered. The shock must have shown on her face.

"I remember a lot of things about you, Nicki."

She closed her eyes against the wave of heartache. She couldn't do this. He was too close, too sexy, just too much. She had to find Nana's chest and get out of there. When she opened her eyes again, she met his gaze. "I remember a lot, too, Randy. But most of all I remember how it felt when you left and never came back."

Nicole tried to head down the hallway but Randy stopped her. "I told you what happened, why I left when I did."

"I heard what you said and I'm sorry for what you went through with your mother. But that doesn't explain why you cut me out of your life so suddenly and completely. And it doesn't change years of hurt." Nicki tried to walk away again.

Once again Randy stopped her. "How can I make it up to you?"

She sighed. "I don't know." She turned her head to meet his gaze. "I don't know if you can." The pleading in his eyes called to something she thought had been long buried. "But for now, you can help me find Nana's chest."

Randy nodded and let go of her arm. She retreated to the safety of the other attic space.

She didn't think about the door being locked until she reached for the handle. She didn't want to have to return to get the key from Randy, because she needed a moment to compose herself. When the handle turned without resistance, she breathed a sigh of relief. The air from the attic cooled her heated body and helped refocus her thoughts on what she needed to do.

Find the chest. Wait for the roads to defrost. Get back to work before Yvonne took over the *Art at Dark* spot.

Nicole poked around the piles in the second attic, trying to find any kind of chest stuck under or between boxes. By the time she finished the first pass, she felt calmer and more in control of her feelings.

"It will take me a month of digging to find that damn chest," she grumbled to the dust and boxes cluttered around her.

"I've got time if you do."

She turned and found Randy standing in the doorway. Much to her irritation, her heart skipped a beat. "I'm sure you'll be needed back in Chicago long before then."

Randy shrugged in a noncommittal way. "You ready to take that break yet?"

When Nicole shook her head and started to protest any delay, Randy continued. "It's cold up here. You need to warm up and eat something. I heated a can of soup for us. It's not much, but it's hot and will keep you going." Randy held his hand out to her, palm up. "Please come down and eat with me, then we'll start looking again."

For some reason, she found it hard to resist the sincerity in his voice and in his eyes.

"I am a little hungry," she admitted.

She took a deep breath then a few steps to the door. Fearing where it might lead her, she hesitantly placed her hand in his.

Randy closed his fingers around hers and gave them a reassuring squeeze then released her. Nicole shivered as she broke eye contact with him and headed to the stairs.

The den stayed warm despite being a large open area. Randy had done a great job keeping the fire going. He must have put the soup on while she looked through the second attic.

After ladling both of them healthy portions into pottery bowls, Randy sat on the floor a foot or two away with his legs stretched out in front of him.

"So, other than a desire to find some long-lost heirlooms that may possibly be valuable artwork, what made you drive all the way out here and risk getting trapped in a snowstorm for the weekend?"

Nicki shifted on the pallet she'd made on the floor near the fireplace. "Nana made me swear that I wouldn't miss *another* family event." She grimaced. "I've missed the last eight or ten, so I couldn't very well refuse."

"Have you been busy at work or have other things been getting in the way?"

"Mostly work. But the reality is, I could have made time if I really wanted to. I just didn't."

"I know what you mean." He took a sip from his soup spoon. "I should have come to Gram and Pop's long before now. I don't usually stay away so long."

"So, why did you?"

Randy lifted one shoulder in response. "I don't know. Maybe I didn't want to think about the answers to the questions I knew they would ask me when I came."

"What questions would those be?"

"Oh, you know. 'Why haven't you found a nice girl and settled down?' or 'When are you going to give up that jet-setting career and have a couple of kids?'"

Nicole nodded her understanding. She received similar questions when her family got together since she was the last of the cousins to marry. And she wasn't even the youngest. "As much as I hate to be asked those questions, why haven't you gotten married and had your required two and a half kids?"

Randy looked into the fire, seemingly lost in his thoughts. "I came close."

Nicole's heart twisted in her chest. Part of her wasn't surprised he'd found someone to marry. The other part cried out in protest. That part didn't want to hear anything about another woman. "I'm sorry. I shouldn't pry," she murmured.

He shrugged. "No, it's fine. She and I figured out before we got too far down the path that we were better off not marrying yet remaining friends." He smiled as he stood, holding the now empty bowl. "Last I heard from her she'd found Mr. Right and planned to have a small wedding and honeymoon in Greece."

Nicole blinked in surprise. He seemed rather casual about his former fiancée getting married. "So you two still talk?"

"Sure." He held out his hand for her bowl. When she handed it to him, he added, "We parted as friends, but who knows? If we'd gotten married, it could have ended in disaster and she might never have met Charles."

"And you're okay with her marrying someone else?"

"Absolutely. Like I said, we realized it wouldn't have worked out. If Charles makes her happy, why wouldn't I be happy for her?"

Huh.

"What about you? Why haven't you ever hooked up and had a dozen pups?" he asked.

Nicole's heart squeezed. She forced a smile. "Oh, you know. The usual reasons. Mr. Right hasn't dropped out of the clear blue sky and I'd rather work than take the time to look for him."

She held Randy's gaze, hoping he didn't see through her flippant remark.

After a moment's hesitation, he said, "I can certainly relate to not having enough time for a personal life. It feels like Vince and I have been going nonstop since we went into business for ourselves." He chuckled. "But then again, that's not much of an excuse, since Vince managed to find the woman of his dreams somewhere along the way. They're expecting their first baby in the next month or two."

Nicole looked away, acting as if it were imperative that she find a blanket, so Randy wouldn't see her expression.

"So, what keeps you so busy at work that you can't look for Mr.

Right?"

Thankful for the change of direction in their conversation, Nicole answered, "Mostly the show, I guess. There's a lot to do to keep up with who the up-and-coming artists are, where the hottest gallery shows will be, and what the trends in the art world are. Then there are the ratings we have to track and reviews we get at the station." Nicole folded her arms across her chest. "It can be a cutthroat business to stay on top of the ratings chart."

"How much competition is there for your show?"

"From other stations? Or from other reporters wanting to take over the show?"

"Other reporters want to take over your show?" Randy's brow raised in question. "From your own station?"

Nicole shrugged. "From other stations, too."

"I didn't realize. So why do you keep doing it? It doesn't sound like much fun if you have to constantly worry about someone taking it over."

"It's the nature of the beast. If I want to stay in this business, I have to play the games. Part of the problem is how popular the segment is, and part of it is who's running the show. Eventually I will get replaced. Something new could come along that sends the station in a different direction or they may decide my ideas have become dated and don't keep up with the times."

"Do your coworkers ever help you out?"

"Some, but not all. I have a couple of camera guys I can rely on no matter what. And there are a few girls around the office who keep me updated with local gossip and news." Nicole stared into the fire. "But then there's Yvonne."

"Yvonne?"

Nicole took a deep breath. "Yeah, Yvonne. She's the head reporter for the entertainment spot." Nicole looked up at Randy with a sheepish expression. "I worked for her as an intern in college then again after I graduated until I came up with the *Art at Dark* spot idea."

"Let me guess, she didn't much care for the attention your show idea got?"

"Not at all. She tried to keep the spot, claiming it belonged under entertainment, but Bob had other ideas. He wanted it to be separate, to follow the governor's *Promote the Art* initiatives."

"Bet that irritated her."

"Yes." Nicole nodded again. "It sure did."

"How long have you been doing the show?"

"The first one ran as a separate spot a little over a year ago."

"I thought it had been longer than that."

Nicole started to respond when it occurred to her to wonder why Randy would know. She stared wide-eyed, not sure what to make of his comment.

Randy caught her expression then ran one hand through his hair, just behind his ear. A nervous gesture she remembered well.

"I, uh, I'm sure Gram or Pop mentioned something about it. It just seems like it was more than a year ago when they did."

Nicole held his gaze, debating whether or not to pursue the thought. "Yeah, well, the idea for the show and the planning started much earlier than that." Nicole rearranged her legs beneath the blanket she had pulled off the couch. She was far more comfortable talking about a subject that didn't dreg up old memories. "We started a little slow. There were a few interviews that ran as part of the entertainment report then we filmed the test shows. We had to convince Bob it would work and that we had a viewership for the spot."

"Obviously he bought in to the idea."

She nodded. "Even I was surprised by the demand for the show. We had several emails saying they were pleased with the direction we were taking and asking for more." Her grin turned sheepish. "Of course it didn't hurt that I'd been spreading the word in the art community and encouraging friends and friends of friends to write in. Artists will do almost anything to get their work in front of an audience."

He pointed one finger at her, emphasizing his first word. "That's the power of marketing."

They shared a smile. The familiar warmth of their old connection trickled through her. It was alarming and comforting at the same time. Unsure how to handle the conflicting emotions, Nicole broke eye contact then moved to sit on the ledge of the fireplace.

"So other than that woman trying to take over your show, it sounds as if you love your job."

"I do." She turned her face toward the fire, thinking about events that had occurred over the last few years. "Actually, I can even deal with Yvonne most days."

"But…"

"But…" She hesitated as she turned to face him. The look of sincerity and interest in his expression overcame her reservations and she gave in to her impulse to be honest about her situation. "Do you know what it's like to wake up one morning and question if where you were in your life and what you were doing was *really* what you wanted?"

"To some degree." He crossed his arms over his chest and stared into the fire. "I love my work. Opening our own business is what Vince and I both wanted to do. I don't regret it for a minute."

"But…" Nicole prompted him like he had done to her.

He grinned. "But I'm definitely not where I'd like to be in my personal life."

"Oh," Nicole said as she exhaled. Once again she found herself torn between wanting to know more and afraid of what he'd say if she asked.

CHAPTER FOURTEEN

Nicki adjusted her position on the ledge of the fireplace. "You know, now that I'm sitting here in this cabin with little heat and no electricity, knowing my recently paid off car might have been squished by a mammoth tree, the things that were stressing me out before I left really don't seem all that annoying now." She looked at Randy. "I feel like a whiner for even bringing it up to Nana and Steve earlier this week."

The mention of another man's name from her lips irritated him. He tried to keep his voice neutral when he asked, "Steve your boyfriend?"

She met his gaze and furrowed her brows in question. "No." She drew out the word. "Steve isn't my boyfriend."

Relief washed over him but curiosity replaced his irritation. Who was Steve and how did he earn enough of Nicki's confidence to be that close to her and to know her grandmother as well? It was on the tip of his tongue to ask, even though he had no right to know. Thankfully Nicky was feeling chatty and he didn't have to.

"Steve's a good friend of mine." She smiled in a way that hinted there was more to her story. "Actually, he's my best friend." She grinned even more. "My BFF."

Randy grunted, not knowing what to say to that.

She got up and moved back to what had become her chair. Once she curled up with the blanket wrapped around her, she explained. "Steve and I met in college. We helped each other through algebra and economics as well as a few rough patches in our lives." She paused as if she were looking back in time. "Steve's parents freaked out when he came clean about being gay during our sophomore year. They even stopped speaking to him. It was a difficult time for him." Nicki looked at Randy as if expecting confirmation.

Randy murmured, "I'm sure it was."

She seemed satisfied with his response and continued her story. "Steve came home with me for Christmas holidays and spring break from then on. After a while we just considered him part of the family."

Randy nodded, relieved to know that even though Steve had a part in her life, it wasn't a romantic part. "Are he and his parents on speaking terms now?"

"Sort of. He talks to his mom fairly regularly now, but not his dad." The sorrow she felt for her friend showed in her eyes.

"At least he had you to lean on when he needed it." Randy remembered several times he wished Nicki had been there for him. It had been his own fault she wasn't. Trying to change his line of thought, he asked, "So what did Steve major in? Was he an art history genius, too?"

Her cheeks turned pink at the compliment. "No, he was a marketing major. Now he works for Claxton & Davis as an ad manager."

Randy let out a low whistle. "He must have done very well in school. I hear it's hard to get into C & D. Even in Chicago they're well known for their innovative ad campaigns."

She nodded. "Oh, yeah, he did really well in school. Magna cum laude. He's the reason I made it through calculus with a B."

"I'll have to remember that next time we need help with advertising. The last firm we worked with was chosen because Vince knew someone related to someone working there. That didn't work out as well as we hoped."

Randy refilled his coffee. He held the pot out in Nicki's direction to ask if she wanted any.

"Sure." She found her mug and handed it to him. "Thanks."

As he poured the coffee, he asked, "So, what about your family? How's your mom?"

"Mom's fine. Don't know how much Rosie has told you over the years, but she remarried a couple of years ago."

Randy replaced the pot on the fireplace ledge. He pushed it close enough to the fire to keep it warm. "Seems like she did say something about it. How's that working out?"

Nicki snorted. "Great for her. Not so great for me."

He took his seat on the floor where he could lean against the ottoman and still face Nicki. "Why would her getting married be not so great for you? You don't live with them, right?"

"No. Thank God," she blurted.

"Aren't you glad she found someone?"

"Yeah, but just because she found the perfect man for her doesn't mean she is qualified to find Mr. Right for me."

Randy hid his chuckle behind his mug. "Is she playing matchmaker?"

Nicki narrowed her eyes in warning and glared at him. "You have no idea."

"Just tell her you're not interested."

"Do you honestly think I haven't?" Nicki crossed her arms in front of her. "I made the mistake of humoring her at first and went out with a couple of the guys. Just dinner or drinks, mind you. But none of them worked out."

"No spark?"

"To say the least. Most of them seemed to be of the same mindset and never called for a second date."

"Most?" Randy asked, already worried about where her story might lead.

Nicki shrugged. "Steve thinks its Mom's fault that I ended up with a stalker."

Randy almost dropped his cup. "You have a what?" he exclaimed as he sat up and leaned toward Nicki.

"Stalker may be too strong of a word."

"What exactly *do* you mean then?" Given the startled expression on Nicki's face, he must have growled his question.

"I keep getting flowers from some anonymous person."

"Okay." He drew out the word. "What makes you think they aren't from a secret admirer?"

"I suppose they could be but the notes are a little too creepy for someone with a romantic interest. And if they are an admirer, I don't want to have anything to do with the weirdo."

"What do the notes say?" Randy's fight reflex kicked in, making his heart beat faster.

"Different things. Usually along the lines of, 'I'm still watching,' or, 'Can't wait to see you again.' Nothing overtly threatening, but creepy enough to make me worry when I walk out to my car at night."

Something stronger than annoyance bubbled up. Someone had scared Nicki, whether they intended to or not, and it he didn't like it. His instinct demanded he hunt the unknown person down and beat some sense into them.

But it isn't my place. She isn't mine.

"Who have you told about the flowers? I hope you at least talked to the police."

She sighed. "Yes, I did talk to a friend of a friend who is an officer. They can't do anything about it is since there is no evidence of a threat."

Randy muttered something rude under his breath.

"I told Bob first. He's the station manager. He thought it might be someone who watches the show. I'm supposed to let him know anytime I receive something. He's the one who had me talk to the police so they at least have a paper trail started."

"A paper trail will do lots of good," he muttered as he got up and began to pace. It certainly wouldn't stop a criminal from attacking her.

From the corner of his eye he saw Nicki shrug. "It may be nothing. It could be a harmless fan who doesn't mean anything malicious."

Her tone of voice hinted she didn't completely believe that however. "Maybe. You said your friend Steve knows about this? And your grandmother?"

"Yeah. Steve's known about it all along. Nana just found out about it this week." She mumbled, "Thanks to Steve's big mouth."

"At least they know to keep an eye out."

"An eye out for what?"

Randy shrugged as he continued to pace, trying to work off some of the frustration he felt at not being able to do anything. "I suppose anything odd." Confusion over why he felt so strongly about the potential danger to Nicki compounded his irritation.

"You mean like strange men leaving phone numbers and messages on my voice mail?"

Randy stopped pacing. "Exactly that."

"Or perhaps you mean strange men showing up unexpectedly with my mother when I give in and agree to meet her for lunch?"

He stared at Nicki in disbelief. "What?"

Nicki rolled her eyes. "Mother has decided that I'm way behind in my efforts to find Mr. Right. She thinks I should find Mr. Okay, settle down, and start producing the grandbabies she wants."

"You must be kidding."

"Do I look like I'm kidding?" she said through gritted teeth. "She's been trying to set me up on blind dates with every unmarried man she's met under the age of sixty."

Randy's jaw dropped.

"The last one I agreed to go out with turned out to be a guy she met at the grocery store when she tipped a display of trash bags on him. Apparently she reached for the box on the top of the pile and, voila! She just knew that fate had sent those boxes tumbling down so that she could introduce us."

If Randy didn't think the potential stalker held some danger for Nicki, he might have thought her mother's efforts were funny. Instead they only made him angrier.

"I told her I wasn't going out on any more of her blind dates, even if she had the Man of the Year lined up, ready to go. So now I get random phone calls from men I don't know. I think she's posted my phone number on a billboard somewhere."

Randy blinked, unable to form a single word. How could her mother be so oblivious to the danger she put her daughter in by handing out Nicki's number to anyone around town? To complete strangers. He struggled to remember everything he could about Nicki's mother, worried that insanity might run in the family. At least Nicki's grandmother always seemed sane.

Knowing it would do no good to yell at Nicki for something her mother had done, he simply remarked, "I can see where that would be annoying." He applauded himself for presenting an outward appearance of calm.

"At least the guys Mother tries to throw my way only call. They don't show up at my apartment."

Randy's hand curled into a fist and he gritted his teeth.

Next time he saw her, Nicki's mother was not going to like what he had to say to her.

CHAPTER FIFTEEN

Nicole watched the play of emotions flit across Randy's face. For a moment it looked as if he wanted to throttle someone. Then again, the fire could have been casting shadows.

Unsure what to make of Randy or her own unsteady emotions, she opted for action. "Since you cooked, I'll clean up." With a flick of her wrist she tossed the blanket back then hopped off the chair. She grabbed her coffee mug and napkin as well as the bowls and spoons they had used for lunch and took them to the kitchen.

She felt Randy's eyes on her as she walked away but refused to turn around. It shouldn't matter to her whether or not he liked what he saw. But it did, dammit.

She dropped the dirty dishes in the sink a little harder than she meant to and turned the water on. Remembering the power had been off all day, she flipped the water off. Over her shoulder she shouted, "Hey, Randy? How long do you think the warm water will last if the power stays off?"

"We'll have plenty of warm water unless one of the water lines freezes," he called from the den.

"How? The power's off."

"Pop installed a gas water heater a few years ago."

"Oh. Well, that's good to know." Nicole flipped the faucet lever to turn the water back on, added some soap, and allowed the sink to fill about halfway. "So, we'll be able to take a bath then?"

"Yeah, but keep in mind the air is going to keep getting colder in the bathroom."

"True." She scrubbed the dishes but left them in the soapy water. "Okay, so maybe just a sponge bath then."

Randy made a choking noise behind her. Nicole looked over

her shoulder at him. "Are you okay?"

"Fine," he rasped out.

Nicole shrugged and finished washing the dishes in the sink. "Do you want me to clean the coffeepot? Or do you think it's okay for now?"

"It's fine for now. I'll grab the pot I used to heat the soup, though."

"Oh, yes. Thanks."

The domestic scene they created made her uneasy. Eight years before, she would have been ecstatic to have Randy to herself for several days. Now, it unsettled her. They were both adults and had known each other since they were children. Logically there was no reason they couldn't stay in the same house.

No reason except the fact that, despite old heartache, she was still attracted to him. She longed to run her fingers through his hair. Her body heated, wondering what she would find if given time to explore his matured and well-taken-care-of body.

"Did you want me to dry those?"

Nicole jerked herself from her errant thoughts. Randy leaned against the counter not far away. "What?" Her face grew warm and she hoped he didn't notice. Her fair complexion tended to give away every thought she had.

If he noticed, he didn't say anything. "Do you want me to dry those?" He tipped his head toward the sink of soapy dishes.

"Um, sure. That'd be great." Nicole rinsed the soap off one of the bowls and handed it to him.

"When we're done, I think I'll check the outside of the cabin again. I want to make sure nothing else has fallen on the house or the road. It'll be dark soon and I don't want to wait until morning."

"That's probably a good idea." Nicole looked out the window. "It's still coming down pretty heavy out there. Do you want me to go with you?"

He shrugged. "You can if you want, but there's no point in both of us getting cold."

"I'd kind of like to check my car."

"All right."

They finished rinsing and drying the dishes and went their separate ways to change clothes. When Nicole returned to the den, Randy was just zipping up his coat. She hadn't noticed before but he wore a very expensive brand of ski jacket. As she slipped her coat over her sweater and turtleneck she noticed his jeans were also a designer brand. Steve had raved about them but complained about how much they cost. *Randy's business must be doing very well.*

She pulled her hat and gloves on, feeling somewhat self-conscious of her mismatched set. Oh well. She might not be able to afford the high-dollar stuff but she did all right. She had her own apartment, she paid her bills each month, and she'd just paid off her car.

Of course, there was now a tree lying on the vehicle.

Just thinking about it made her want to cry.

"You ready?" Randy asked.

She took a deep breath to prepare herself. "Yeah. Let's go."

Randy had pulled on one of those old-fashioned hats with flaps that covered his ears. Something about it struck her as familiar. He must have noticed the questioning look on her face, because he said, "It's one of Pops' hats. I've always liked it." He grinned. "What do you think? Is it me?"

She swallowed a laugh. "Oh, it's definitely you." Trying to keep a straight face, she suggested, "Come on. Let's see what's going on out there before it gets any later."

He unlatched the locks on the front door and, with a sweeping gesture, opened it and bowed slightly. "After you."

Nicole shook her head and crossed her arms over her chest. "Uh-uh. You just want to see if I'll fall on my butt. I'll let you see how slick the porch steps are."

"You always were a fast learner, weren't you? How about we go together?"

She almost said yes but changed her mind. Despite how pretty the fresh snow made everything, there was bound to be a hidden layer of ice beneath. "No way. If either of us go down, we'll take the other with us. Then we'd both end up with a busted butt or sprained ankle. I think I'll just work my way down on my own."

"You're probably right. Okay. Here I go." He scooted to the edge of the porch then grabbed the handrail and slowly made his way down the steps.

She followed the same path and manner Randy had taken then took Randy's outstretched hand when she reached the last couple of steps. Once they were standing on the ground, despite the layer of ice, they were able to walk with only a small measure of caution.

Snow trickled down in large, thick flakes. She had to blink to keep the frozen particles from sticking to her eyelashes when she looked up at the treetops and roofline.

"I'm going to check the east side of the cabin," he told her.

"All right." The ice crunched beneath her boots as she walked to the front of her car. She choked back a whimper when she saw how many limbs covered it.

Her poor car.

Randy had been right. She had gotten lucky. The tree trunk missed the bumper by inches but there were a lot of branches that hadn't. "As long as nothing is broken, it should be fine," she muttered to herself. "A little buffing. Maybe a little paint and it'll be good."

When she reached the other side, she squatted to look under the branches that lay across the hood. It didn't look as if anything had been dented and there were no metal pieces hanging loose that she could see. So that was good.

She stood from her crouching position and saw something whizz by in a blur of white. Startled, she looked around and barely had time to duck before something else came zipping past. The second projectile narrowly missed the top of her head.

A snowball lay splattered nearby.

Randy. That devil.

She laughed and ducked behind her car.

A sneak attack. Randy and her cousin Jacob used to pull them all the time.

"Oh, you are so dead, Stephenson!" she shouted. "You still haven't learned how to make a proper snowball."

"Oh yeah?"

"Yeah." She gathered snow and packed it into a ball. Then another and another as more than one snowball sailed over the top of her car. When she had several pieces of ammunition she crept to the back edge and took a peek to see if she could find his hiding spot. She found him at the edge of the porch just before he tossed another snowball. She ducked behind the car and the ball splattered against the bumper. She looked around for a better area to launch her attack.

The large tree on the other side of the circle drive would do. It had plenty of snow nearby for making more ammo.

She made a few more snowballs then gathered up everything she could carry and dashed for cover.

One snowball whirled past her but a second caught her on the shoulder before she reached the tree. Once there, she had a perfect view of Randy, because he had no shelter from this new angle.

She dropped her supplies and began firing at will. She thought she was doing well until he charged at her.

"Now you're in for it."

Nicole squealed and ran to her car. She didn't have time to reach her first batch of snowballs before Randy grabbed her and toppled them both into the snow.

Laughing harder than she had in years, she tried to wrestle free, but Randy rolled her beneath him, effectively pinning her. Their laughter died as they stared into each other's eyes. Randy held her gaze as he slowly lowered his head and touched his lips to hers. Confusion set in from the heat that rippled through her body despite the snow beneath her. Desire warred with her better sense. The lost years and the hurt melted away in an instant.

Randy stopped long enough for her to see his shocked yet wary expression. Hers likely mirrored his. His next kiss was deeper and longer than the first. Their tongues touched and teased each other and soon she clung to him, nearly senseless.

When they stopped, they were both panting, but it wasn't due to their brief chase.

"Nicki, I—"

Self-preservation sprang to life despite the fluttery sensations zipping through her body. "We can't do this." Nicole scrambled to get up out of the snow. She wiped the few strands of hair away from her face and touched her lips. The cold and wet that clung to her gloves were a sharp contrast.

"Nicki, don't—"

She held up her hand to halt his advance. "Stop. Just give me a minute." She backed toward the cabin.

Randy regarded her. "All right." He wiped the snow off his jeans and jacket. "I'm going to finish checking the outside of the cabin. Why don't you go on inside and warm up?"

She snorted. As if she wasn't already overheated. "That's probably a good idea."

When she made it inside, she closed the heavy door and leaned against it. God. No one affected her as much as Randy with just a kiss. That much hadn't changed in the last eight years.

What the hell was she going to do with him now?

CHAPTER SIXTEEN

Randy checked the area behind the cabin but very little of what he saw registered with him. His thoughts were inside with Nicki.

Kissing her had been a mistake. If he wanted to get back into her good graces, he needed to move slower.

Why was she so skittish? It wasn't as if they'd never kissed before.

Granted, no one ever turned him inside out the way she did.

Even after all this time he knew he could spend hours, maybe even days, doing nothing but exploring her lips. He used to think the feeling had been due to a first-love thing. But no, that feeling remained after all this time. If nothing else, it had been magnified now that he'd sampled many of the world's charms and found them lacking.

He ended up at Pop's wood-splitting pile. Looking out onto the valley, he realized why Pop spent so much time there. Even covered with a blanket of white, the view was spectacular.

He had stayed away too long.

He turned back to the house. The flickering candlelight in the den window beckoned.

At the back porch he stamped the snow off his boots. He paused at the door, uncertain of what he might find inside. Nicki had fled but he wondered which she feared more, him or herself. He needed to find out.

Inside, he hung his coat on the hook then stepped around the corner. Nicki sat next to the fire. "You get warm yet?"

She looked over her shoulder in his direction. "Mostly. You were out there a while." She stood and gestured where she had been sitting. "You should probably get next to the fire so you can warm up."

Like a nervous cat, she moved away as he drew closer.

"I didn't realize how cold I was until I came in." He held his hands out toward the fire.

Nicki curled up at one end of the couch and wrapped the blanket around her. "Everything all right out there?"

"As far as I could tell, yes."

"Good. Can't afford any more mishaps."

"A mishap like that kiss?"

"That was a mistake."

He turned to face her. "Why? Seemed pretty natural to me."

She clutched the blanket closer. "Doesn't mean it should happen again."

"If we both liked it, why not?"

She narrowed her eyes. "I like Rocky Road ice cream. Doesn't mean it's good for me or that I should indulge in it just because it's in my freezer."

He grinned. "Still have a thing for chocolate and marshmallows, huh?"

She lifted her chin a notch. "Actually I prefer strawberry these days."

"You look good in pink," he murmured.

Nicki leapt to her feet. "Just stop it. How can you sit there and pretend that you want me now when eight years ago I wasn't nearly good enough for you?"

Randy came to his feet. "What the hell are you talking about?"

"You! You're sitting here hitting on me even though you made it perfectly clear you wanted nothing more to do with me back then. What do I look like to you? An idiot?" The blanket fluttered to the ground as her hands flailed around during her rant. "You must think I'm some kind of desperate fool to get involved with you right now. Just because there's no one else to pick from doesn't mean I'm going to fall at your feet and beg you to sleep with me. I'm sure you've got all kinds of women back in Chicago for that."

He grabbed her by the arms to stop her pacing and capture her attention. "Let's get one thing clear. I'm not hitting on you because there is no one else here. I am still attracted to you. That kiss only proved how much. And yes, I have been with my fair share of women over the years, but none measured up to you or to what we had together." He took a deep breath and released her. "The truth is, I've missed you."

"You've missed me?" she asked incredulously. "You walked away more than eight years ago and never looked back. How can you sit there and say you missed me?"

Randy ran a hand through his hair. "Yes, I did walk away from you. From us," he amended. "But you have no idea how often I did look back. And how sorry I am that I left the way I did."

"You were always a smart guy. Don't tell me that you expected to come here, apologize, and just pick up where we left off."

"Of course not. But—"

"No buts. That's just not happening." She folded her arms across her chest. "When you left without saying good-bye, you broke my heart." Tears pooled in her eyes. "I was young and foolishly in love with you. And you had to know it."

Randy reached for her hand and tried to tug her toward him, but she resisted.

"I did know it," he admitted. "And I knew how much. That's part of what scared me."

"Scared you?"

"Yes, I was scared." He let go of her hand and walked to the fireplace.

Randy leaned against the stone on one elbow and rested his forehead on the meaty side of his arm as he stared down into the flames. "I know it may not make much sense to you. You always seemed to know what you wanted to do with your life. But not me. It wasn't until after Mom died that I sorted out what I wanted to do with my life."

He lifted his head and looked Nicole in the eye. "I had nothing to offer you then, Nicki. Nothing. I knew you loved me and I knew you would have followed me to Chicago or wherever I went. And I loved you enough to *not* ask that of you."

He turned to face her fully. "When I got the call that Mom was sick, they told me she was in the advanced stages of cancer. They were also very clear it would be a bumpy ride from there out." He jammed his hands into the pockets of his jeans. "I had no idea how I would manage school and a job so I could pay for the medical expenses I knew she'd have."

"Oh, Randy. Why didn't you just tell me all of this back then?" Nicole asked as she sank onto the edge of the couch.

"What would it have changed? I didn't want to submit you to that kind of life, so why make you worry?"

"But—"

"It doesn't matter now." He shrugged. "I did what I thought I needed to do and I can't take it back." He added quietly, "I'm just sorry that I hurt you. Despite the time we've been apart, I've never forgotten you and how I felt when we were together."

He closed the distance between them and squatted in front of her. "There were many times when I wished I'd had you beside me." He tapped her lightly on the nose. "And I don't mean just during the difficult times."

He smiled. "I thought of you as I got that first big promotion, wondering what you'd think of where I'd landed. You were on my mind as I crossed the stage when I got my bachelor's. With honors, I might add. And so many other times, I've lost track."

Nicki sniffed and swallowed. "You could have called or written, you know."

"I know. And I did, in the beginning."

She blinked but her expression of surprise quickly turned to disbelief.

He put one hand on her knee. "I didn't say I mailed the letters." He shrugged one shoulder. "I could never quite get the words right to tell you everything I wanted, so I kept them."

"Harrumph," Nicole murmured.

"Before long, I convinced myself that you had gotten over your hurt and moved on in life. I figured Mr. Right was on your horizon, so I went looking for Mrs. Right. But no matter how hard I tried, everyone I dated ended up not working out. Then sometime this last summer I realized it was because I kept comparing all these women to you."

"But Randy, you don't know me anymore. I'm not the same person I was eight years ago."

"That's probably true." He nodded in agreement. "I know I'm not the same person I was eight years ago. But I think I knew the real you, the one deep down inside that probably never changes. The part you don't show most people. The part that makes you tick and makes you who you are."

He pressed his palm against Nicki's cheek. "I felt something when we were together. Something I haven't felt with anyone else. I had already made up my mind that I needed to see you again. I wanted to know if that feeling was real or if I had made it larger than life."

Nicki blinked back a fresh set of tears. "I don't know what to say, Randy."

"I don't expect you to say anything." He leaned back onto his heels, giving her some space. "I'm just telling you the truth." He stood then pushed his hands into his pockets. "When I saw you here at the cabin, I knew I needed to find out if you hated me for leaving and if I had a chance to change your mind."

She looked up. "I don't hate you. I never did." She rubbed her hands across the tops of her thighs. "I don't know how I feel right now, other than I'm afraid you being here means I'm going to leave with another broken heart."

"I know it's late in coming, but I'm sorry. I'm sorry for the way I left, for not sending any of the letters, for not contacting you over the years. But most of all, I'm sorry I ever caused you any pain."

Before Nicole could respond, the lights clicked on in the kitchen and the heater sparked to life.

"The power is back on." Randy smiled. "Maybe that's a sign that someone is pulling for me and knows I can use all the help I can get."

CHAPTER SEVENTEEN

Randy must have sensed her need for some distance. Right after the power came on, he bundled up and went outside to make sure nothing sparked from any of the power lines around the cabin. Nicole was grateful for the time alone. He had given her a lot to think about and it was distracting having him nearby.

She couldn't deny their physical attraction. Every time she looked at him, her fingers itched to touch him and she had flashbacks to one of the last times they had made love. She shook off the thrill that zinged down her spine, wondering what it would be like to be with him now.

Coffee.

She should fix coffee.

Randy did a good job improvising with the campfire coffee this morning, but she craved a cup of her favorite morning brew. And Randy would need something warm when he came back inside.

She quickly prepared what she needed then hovered nearby, waiting not so patiently for the pot to fill. Spotting the remote to the TV sitting on the counter, she clicked on the power, hoping to catch the news on the weather and road conditions.

Randy came through the rear entrance just as she found one of the local stations. He hung his coat on the peg next to the door and dropped his hat and gloves on the floor below his coat.

"What did they say about the roads?" he asked.

"I just turned it on, so nothing yet."

Nicole remained at her post in the kitchen near the coffee while Randy crossed the room and sat on the fireplace ledge. "Everything still okay out there?"

"I heard a couple of tree branches snap but it was most likely smaller ones that couldn't hold the weight of the ice. I didn't see anything to be alarmed about."

Nicole nodded. "Good. You think the power will stay on?"

"If it goes off again, it shouldn't be because of the lines on the property. It'll be a bigger problem back at the main road." Randy peeled his sweater off and laid it over the arm of the nearby chair. "Either way, the heater should have the cabin back to a comfortable temperature soon."

"Thank God."

The coffee finished brewing as they watched the rest of the news in silence. She poured two large cups and took one to Randy.

"Thanks." He held her gaze briefly before turning his attention to the TV.

Finally the news returned to road closings. They reported the main highway across the lake to the peninsula had been shut down. The jackknifed truck that had caused the road closure damaged part of the bridge railing. With the ice and snow, highway officials felt it would be safer to close the bridge until they could get a repair crew in. It would be another day or two before it would reopen.

If she decided to brave the icy roads to get home before that bridge reopened, she would add a minimum of a couple hours to her drive time. The only other way off the peninsula was a route that would take her most of the way around the lake in the opposite direction. Driving on unfamiliar lake roads while they were iced over and hard to navigate did not appeal to her at all.

In addition, the highway patrol advised anyone who didn't have to be on the roads to stay indoors for the next day or two.

So her present situation boiled down to her car being buried under a tree with uncertain damages, a gravel drive leading to the main road with questionable conditions, a bridge closure blocking her direct route off the peninsula, icy roads, and warnings from the highway patrol saying drivers should stay home. Oh, and she still hadn't found the paintings she wanted.

There was no way around it. She was stuck here for a couple of days.

With Randy.

A tiny flare of panic made her heart skip. But to her surprise, a warm, fluttery sensation between her legs quickly replaced her panic.

What if… She bit her lip and allowed her thoughts free reign.

What if she used this time to prove to herself that she had gotten over him? What if she gave in to her body's cravings to feel him once more? Maybe even two or three times. She grinned. What if *she* walked away at the end of the weekend?

Randy said he'd missed her and regretted the way he had walked away, but that didn't mean he had any intention of picking up where they'd left off. He'd be returning to Chicago and the life he built there. Even if she had fallen into some kind of alternate universe and he *did* want to renew their relationship, it wouldn't be possible while he lived in Chicago and she lived in Springfield. Long-distance romances never worked. It would be better to call this what it was up front and spare the heartache down the road.

"Nicki, are you okay?"

The sound of Randy's voice jerked her from her thoughts. "Yeah, why?"

"Because when I asked you a question, you didn't answer and you looked like you were a million miles away."

"Sorry. I was thinking about something." She quickly added, "Something about work."

Her face warmed. It seemed as if Randy had a sixth sense that told him every time she had a sexual thought about him. "What did you ask?"

"I wondered what kind of coffee this was." He held up a mug. "I've never tasted anything like it."

She smiled. "It probably is more frou-frou than anything you're used to. It's a morning blend that I get at a little coffee and tea shop down in the art district. A friend of mine owns it. She mixes and grinds the beans herself." She took a sip, then it occurred to her that he might not like the blend. "I can pour it into another container if you want to make a pot of regular coffee."

"No, it's fine." He took another sip. "Don't know if I'd want it all day, but it's not bad."

"I like it as a wake up in the morning or a pick-me-up in the afternoon to keep me going at work."

"It seems to have a nice caffeine jolt."

She nodded. "Yeah, but it's not as bad as the one she calls 'Powerhouse.'"

"Bet Vince would like that one."

She curled her feet beneath her on the couch. "Vince is your business partner, right?"

"Yes, and he's a total caffeine junkie. I think half of our monthly food-related expenses are for coffee."

She laughed. "Wow."

"He's a runner and a health-food freak. Coffee is his only vice. I'm convinced that's how he won the last marathon he participated in. His morning cup, which is huge, by the way, gave him an edge over everyone else."

"Maybe so," she murmured. Using the remote, she checked the time on the TV display. A little past four. "Think we should risk a power failure and cook dinner on the stove?"

"Might as well." Randy got up and headed to the kitchen. "Even if it cuts out before we're done, we can try to finish it over the fire. Worst case, we might have to stick it in the fridge until we can finish cooking it after the power returns."

Nicole followed him to the kitchen. "I went through a few of the containers in the fridge. Rosie must have been cooking up a storm."

"Good thing."

"Did I tell you thank you yet?"

Randy stopped searching the refrigerator and looked her way. "No, but feel free to start any minute now."

The heat in his gaze sent goose bumps down both of her arms. "Thank you." She stepped closer so she could lay her hand on his arm that rested across the top of the open refrigerator door. "I appreciate what you've done to keep us warm and fed. It would have been a lot scarier if I had been out here alone."

"You're welcome."

"I, uh—" She stopped before she said anything embarrassing. Something like, "I don't know what I'd have done without you," or, "I can think of other ways to get warm that don't require thermals." Instead she took the coward's way out and changed the subject. "So, what can we throw together for dinner?"

They reviewed their options and settled on something that looked easy to heat without messing up a lot of dishes. After their bellies were full, they turned the TV on to a popular sitcom and settled into their respective spots near the fire.

Despite her excitement over the paintings, it didn't make much for Randy to talk her out of going to the attics again until morning. She was warm and drowsy and didn't feel much like getting cold and dusty before bed.

Besides, there was a lot they needed to do tomorrow. Between the tree and the paintings, they would have little time to lounge. At least they had heat again and could warm up in between work sessions.

She only half listened to the television program. Most of her thoughts danced around old memories. She wrestled with the thought that he never knew about the baby she lost. Should she tell him?

Part of her felt he should know. But what good would it do to tell him? There was nothing he could do about it now.

Even if she had been able to reach him eight years ago, there would have been nothing he could have done then either. Nothing except hold her hand and offer comfort.

Eventually her thoughts turned to more pleasant things. When she dozed off she dreamed of Randy and warm summer nights.

CHAPTER EIGHTEEN

When morning broke, Randy stretched and rose from his place on the couch. He said a prayer of thanks that the electricity stayed on through the night.

He and Nicki had both fallen asleep in the den. Despite the lumps in the cushions he slept on, he'd been hesitant to move to the bedroom in case they lost power again. And since he didn't dare lay a hand on Nicki for fear he wouldn't want to stop touching her, he let her sleep in her chair.

He'd enjoyed catching up with her over dinner and hearing about the things he'd missed in her life, but as it had grown later the television made a welcome distraction. He struggled to keep his hands to himself.

More than once he'd caught her glancing his way with a strange look in her eye. One minute he thought he'd become her favorite dessert. The next minute he had the feeling she developed a cavity. It was damned confusing and made him unsure how to proceed.

Then again, Nicki would never fall into his arms crying, "Take me, Randy! I've missed you so." Nothing about Nicki had ever been that simple or straightforward. It was one of the things he'd loved about her. She'd always kept him on his toes.

He rolled his options around as he ambled to the kitchen to find something for breakfast. He put away the clean pots and utensils from dinner then pulled a few things from the fridge. Once he had a couple of ideas of how to deal with her, he set the coffeemaker to brew.

Like the pied piper, the smell of coffee roused Nicki. She stumbled into the kitchen and mumbled, "Good morning."

"Good morning, yourself. Did you sleep okay in that chair?"

She shrugged as she rummaged around in a cabinet for a cup. "Mostly. I was warm. That was all I cared about."

He chuckled. "It's still coming down out there but at least it's just snow now."

She looked toward the kitchen window. "Good. Any chance we could start working to get that tree off my car?"

"Maybe. Let's wait and see if it lets up first."

The noise she made sounded like a cross between a growl and a whimper.

Before the coffee could finish filling the container, she pulled the pot out of the way and placed her mug beneath the dripping java. She lifted the pot, offering what little it held to him. He chuckled and shook his head. "Unlike some people, I can wait until it finishes brewing."

"Your loss." When her cup was nearly full she returned the pot to its rightful place then walked away sipping.

He cut sections out of the breakfast casserole he found in the fridge and put them on a plate in the microwave. When they were warm he carried one to Nicki then sat on the couch to enjoy his portion.

"Thank you," she mumbled as she took his offering.

"So, what do you plan to do first today? The tree or the paintings?" he asked.

She dug in to her breakfast. "The paintings, I think. At least until the sun has had a chance to break through."

He nodded his agreement. "I may get Pop's four-wheeler out and drive up to the road to see if any other trees came down."

Nicki's eyes widened. "I hadn't thought of that. Good idea."

Randy finished his casserole then got up to get another piece. As he waited for the microwave to finish, Nicki brought her plate to the kitchen and rinsed it in the sink.

"Do you need anything from the big bathroom? I was going to take a quick shower."

His heart skipped a beat at the thought of Nicki naked. "Nah. I left my shaving kit in the bedroom, so I'm fine. I'll use the half bath to clean up while you do that."

"Okay."

The microwave dinged as he watched her trudge toward the bedrooms. He took his food out then ate it while he leaned against the kitchen cabinets. All the while he tried to not think about what

Nicki might be doing at the other end of the cabin. When he was finished he rinsed his plate then headed to find his things.

He rushed through his morning ritual but skipped the shave, thinking the stubble might help keep his face warm while he worked outside. He dug through the clothes he brought then rummaged through the things he'd left in one of the dressers. It held mostly summer clothes but he did manage to find an old pair of jeans and one of Pop's flannel shirts. He dressed then went in search of an old work coat and hat and gloves.

After locating the barn key, he shuffled his way out the back to see what Mother Nature had dumped on them.

It took a little effort to open the larger barn door, but the four-wheeler started with only a minor protest. He drove it around the house to warm the engine and make sure it stayed running before taking off for the main road.

If it hadn't been so cold, the air on his face might be refreshing. In truth it made his breath catch.

Other than the occasional gust of wind, the drive to the road was easy, and it helped him focus on something other than his reaction to being near Nicki. Without a doubt, he wanted her physically. As a girl she'd been beautiful, but as a woman she was earthy and sensual. And his body responded every time he looked her way.

But his reaction was more than physical. He wanted to know everything about her. Everything that had changed her from the girl he knew before into the woman she was today.

By the time he reached the highway, he knew what he wanted. He wanted a chance with Nicki. To prove that they were good together. He wanted to make up for lost time and for hurting her. But he wasn't going to get that chance out here, by himself.

At the gate he took a minute to check the condition of the main road then turned the ATV around and headed back to the cabin. There were no other fallen trees on or near the road. And the gravel beneath the snow ensured it remained passable. He felt better knowing if they had an emergency, they could get out. But that meant once the tree was off Nicki's car, she'd be able to leave.

The idea of pulling another tree down sparked to life but he quickly dismissed it. As much as he wanted more time with Nicki, he couldn't bring himself to cheat to get it. He needed to deal with her honestly if he wanted to win her back.

He returned the four-wheeler to the barn then located the chain saw and the other tools he needed to work on the tree. After making sure the chain saw would start, he returned to the cabin.

When he didn't locate Nicki anywhere on the main floor he headed upstairs.

He was pleased she'd taken his advice and hauled one of the small electric heaters upstairs with her. He followed the extension cord down the narrow hallway to the attic on the far end. The walkway connecting the two ends of the upper floor had warmed due to the heat rising from the den; however, the end of the corridor was cold where she had left the attic door open.

When he stepped into the room, he almost tripped over the little heater as his train of thought derailed. All of his blood went rushing to one particular part of his body when he found Nicki leaning over an oversized camelback trunk. Her sweatpants were stretched across her perfectly rounded ass, making Randy question if she wore anything underneath. If she did, there couldn't be much to it, because there were no panty lines. His imagination took off like a rocket as he ran through a list of possibilities: pink, lacy thong, silky white string-thing or even just a little piece of red lace. Each idea made his jeans fit a bit more snug.

"What are—" Randy cleared his throat, trying to get some moisture back to it. "What are you doing?"

Her voice was muffled since half of her upper body was behind the trunk. "I dropped the key and I can't…" She struggled to reach farther. "Can't quite…" Her legs flailed as she strained in her efforts. "…get it."

Randy couldn't take his eyes off Nicki's backside as she wiggled farther over the top of the trunk. Images of her wiggling as he mounted her from behind assaulted him. He took a ragged breath to center himself. "Let me try," he said in a rush.

She pushed herself up and turned around, taking her butt out of his primary line of sight. "I thought I could reach it without moving anything." She slid the rest of the way down the front of the trunk and stepped aside. "But I guess not."

Randy grunted in response. Reaching over the top with the raging hard-on he now sported would be uncomfortable, but what else could he do? "You're going to need to look behind it anyway, right?"

"Yes. Unless the writing chest is inside."

Randy grunted again then wondered if he sounded like a caveman. He pulled the heavier-than-expected antique a few inches and thought of the most nonsexual thing he could to ease some of the stiffness in his jeans. Nicki standing less than two feet away didn't help his concentration. Or lack of.

Taking care to not injure anything, he leaned over the curved top and located the key. Nicki's attempts to reach for it had wedged the end under one of the nearby boxes, but Randy managed to pull it out without moving anything else. He stood then handed the key to Nicki. He let the tips of his fingers slide against her open palm.

Nicki's lips parted and she blushed. If he hadn't been watching for her reaction, he might have missed it. At least he could still affect her with an innocent touch. Perhaps his hopes were not futile.

He nodded to the trunk. "Let's see what's in there."

She cleared her throat. "Yeah."

Randy held his ground between Nicki and the trunk, forcing her to squeeze past him to get to the lock. Despite his own discomfort at her closeness, he wanted to know what she would do.

She ducked her head as she brushed against him but wouldn't look up. He could see enough of the side of her face to tell she had turned a deeper shade of pink.

Just to push things, he remained in his place as she squatted to unlock it. He knew it put his crotch at her eye level and if she turned her head, she would see the unmistakable bulge in the front of his jeans.

Her hand shook a little, causing her to fumble with the key in the lock. He'd bet money her calm demeanor was just a facade.

It took a moment, but the old lock finally cooperated. He helped her slide the trunk forward so the lid would open far enough and not slam shut on her.

The faint smell of mothballs permeated the air. Randy wouldn't have been surprised to find a layer of dust. He squatted next to Nicki to look at the contents.

She glanced at him from the corner of her eye. He couldn't tell if she was surprised or uncomfortable by his nearness. She scooted over a couple of inches then turned and asked, "Any idea what's in here?"

Her discomfort made him grin. "Nope, but let's find out."

She shot another look in his direction. "You know you don't have to stay up here if you don't want to. I can sift through all this junk on my own."

"I know. But I'm curious about what Gram has stashed away up here."

She lifted the thin layer of paper that covered the things stored inside and set it aside. The paper was old enough that it looked as if it might disintegrate if handled too much. Under the paper lay an ivory-colored lace dress.

"Oh my." Nicki sighed in awe. She stood, lifting the dress out of the trunk.

Given the length, it had to have been someone's wedding dress.

"I wonder whose dress this was."

Randy shook his head. "I have no idea. Gram told me and Brian years ago if we messed with that trunk, she'd wear us out." He chuckled at the memory. "If that is Gram's dress, it's fifty years old."

"It's beautiful. I'll have to ask her sometime where it came from." Nicki refolded the dress with care and placed it on top of the paper she had set on the floor.

Next came a few lace things like what he remembered seeing on the coffee tables of elderly aunts. There were a few baby clothes and shoes and what looked like handkerchiefs.

Eventually they came across something of interest to him. Toward the bottom lay a faded green jacket with military patches. "I bet this belonged to Great-Granddad," Randy speculated. When he lifted the jacket, an old revolver, still in its leather holster, fell into the trunk.

"Is that a gun?" Nicki asked as she leaned closer to look.

"It was probably his service weapon." Randy laid the jacket across his lap then reached for the gun. "I'm no expert, but based on the age and wear of the leather, I think that's a safe assumption. Plus it was folded inside the jacket." He inspected the weapon as Nicki dug through the clothes and linens.

When she'd removed the last layer of clothing, she remarked, "The only things left are what looks like a scrapbook, a few books, and some kind of box."

Randy re-holstered the gun and set it aside with the jacket so he could look into the trunk. "I bet that's the writing chest you were looking for," he said as he pointed to the box at Nicki's end of the container.

"You think so? It's pretty small."

"The ones I've seen at auction haven't been very big. They were made so people could travel with them." He invaded Nicki's space once more and deliberately let his shoulder brush across her breast. "Here, I'll get that out." He smiled to himself, pleased to hear Nicki's swift intake of breath. The flush across her cheeks added to his satisfaction.

She definitely wasn't immune to his touch.

"I have a suggestion."

"What's that?" Her voice had a catch to it.

"How about if I carry this downstairs for you? We can go through it where it's warmer and more comfortable."

"What about the rest of this stuff?" Nicki asked.

"We need to repack Gram's things. She'd kill us if we left them out or messed any of them up."

"No kidding," Nicki mumbled.

"It won't take long to repack the clothing. You've been up here a while, though, and should go warm up."

"It *is* a little chilly," she agreed. "Even with the heater going."

"I put a fresh pot of coffee on before I came up," Randy added just to push the envelope.

Nicki looked at the box sitting between them and the clothes on the floor. She was obviously torn between wanting to know immediately if the paintings were in there or not and waiting to find out when they returned to the den.

"I'm just as anxious as you to explore some more, but you don't need to catch a cold by sitting up here freezing."

"Okay," she finally agreed. "Let's put this stuff back."

Randy smiled to himself. "Good." While he liked the close quarters that the attic provided, he wanted Nicki to relax and strip off a layer of clothing. Or two or three. That wasn't going to happen in a cold attic.

Once he had her bundled up in front of the fire again, he'd have to figure out how to warm her up to the idea of sharing his bed. After all, where a woman shared her body, her heart was likely to follow.

91

CHAPTER NINETEEN

By the time Nicole got downstairs, she was a fumbling mess. It seemed as if every time she turned around, Randy was right there, touching her. They were light, seemingly innocent touches. At least they had been at first, but they were becoming far too frequent to be unplanned.

Whatever he was trying to do was driving her mad.

Her body was on fire. Any minute now she was going to throw him to the ground and have her wicked way with him.

Which is probably what he wanted anyway, damn him.

The sane part of her brain that told her what a terrible idea it would be to sleep with Randy was getting harder to hear. She could barely remember why she should resist. After all, it would only be for the weekend.

"Where do you want this?"

Nicole started at the sound of Randy's voice behind her. She realized she'd stopped right in the middle of the den.

"I guess just put it there." She pointed to a spot on the floor near the pallet of pillows she'd left beside the chair. She watched the muscles play across Randy's back and shoulders as he set the chest on the floor near her feet.

When he stood, their eyes met and held. She forgot to blank out her expression. She forgot everything except what it felt like to be held in a man's arms as if she were the most precious thing in the world. Before she knew what was happening, Randy reached out and gently touched her cheek.

The look on his face nearly broke through the remainder of her defenses.

"I, uh…" She pulled away and looked down at the wooden

chest before she betrayed anything. "Thanks for bringing that down."

"Nicki—"

She moved to the fireplace and held her hands out to warm them near the flames. Yes, they were cold, but it was more of an excuse to put space between them. "So how were the roads? Any other trees down?"

He removed his coat and hat and dropped them onto the chair near the front door. "No more trees that I could see. The road was clear all the way to the highway."

"Good." She hopped up when she realized he was heading in her direction. "How about if I get us both some coffee? I'm kinda hungry, too. Are you ready for lunch? I am." She all but ran to the safety of the kitchen.

Randy hesitated before responding. "It's a little early for lunch."

Her instinct demanded she put some distance between her and Randy. The foolish, romantic side of her wanted to fall into Randy's arms and pretend it would all be okay. It terrified her to know the foolish side was winning.

Before she could even refill the grounds in the coffeemaker, Randy joined her and crowded her personal space, setting her nerves ablaze again.

"I can bring your coffee to you in the den," Nicole hinted, hoping he'd give her a few more moments to gather her wits.

"No, that's okay. I'm looking for something to drink that doesn't involve caffeine."

"I think there's some juice in the freezer. Might take a bit to thaw before you can drink it, though." She tried again to shoo him out of the kitchen. "I can start thawing it for later if you want to go on back to the den."

Randy closed in on her. "You know, I'm beginning to think you don't want me in the kitchen." He backed her into the corner of the L-shaped counter, one hand on either side. "Now why is that?"

Nicole's heart sped up. She leaned back as far as she could without looking like she avoided him. The warmth of his body contrasted with the cool tile counter behind her. She wanted to close the gap between them in order to soak up his warmth and feel the hard planes of his form that would fit oh so nicely against her own softer curves.

"I… I don't know what you mean," she stammered. She

couldn't look him in the eye. His lips, so close to her own, captured her attention.

His voice dipped an octave. "Oh, I think you do, Nicki."

Nicole leaned closer. It felt as if there were a magnet inside each of them that had lined up perfectly and pulled the two of them together.

"Nicki," he groaned. "You can't keep looking at me and expect me to not kiss you."

She lifted her gaze to meet his. The naked desire she saw was her undoing. Even if all he wanted from her was a wild weekend of rekindled desire, she would be willing to risk being burned. It had been far too long since she felt this way for a man. To be honest, she couldn't remember experiencing anything remotely close to this intensity with anyone else. It would be worth the risk to her heart just to feel the flames once more. "What if I want you to kiss me?"

Randy growled low in his throat and she felt the tension around him ratchet up a notch. "Then you need to understand that I won't stop with one kiss." He leaned closer, his body only a breath away from hers. "There will be another and another and eventually you will find yourself naked beneath me."

A shiver of excitement rippled through her body at the image he painted in her head.

"Are you sure you're ready for that, Nicki? Because if you're not, you need to run, right now."

Nicole swallowed the last of her fear and put her hands on Randy's waist as she continued to hold his gaze. "Kiss me. Don't let me think about what used to be anymore."

He closed the distance between them and fused his lips to hers. The years of pain and heartache fell away. Nicole felt as if she had stepped into an inferno as passion ignited within her.

She slid her hands under his shirt to feel the muscles of his back and pressed closer. The counter digging into her ribs barely registered with her as she accepted his weight against her.

This was what had been missing from all of the relationships she'd had in the last few years. The unyielding passion. The drowning in sensation so overpowering that you cannot think of your own name.

His mouth ravaged hers and she wanted to cry from the joy of it. The occasional scrape of teeth didn't even bother her as they fought for control of the kiss. She wanted to consume all of him.

She wanted to be consumed by him. She needed more. She needed him.

His hand had slipped beneath her shirt and pushed her bra out of the way. He caressed and teased her breast until her nipple became a hard pebble. She longed to feel his chest pressed against hers. The warmth. The solid feel of him.

Randy picked her up and sat her on the edge of the counter then fit himself between her legs. Even with their clothes as a barrier, she could feel his erection pressing against her. It fueled her desire further.

Nicole let herself become lost in the flood of sensations he created. She didn't realize he had unbuttoned her flannel shirt until he pushed the fabric off her shoulders. Annoyed by the barrier between them, she pulled her hands from the sleeves then broke their kiss long enough for him to pull her thermal undershirt over her head.

The cool air reached her bare skin and she tried to move back into the warm circle of Randy's arms. He held her by the waist and prevented her from scooting closer as he gazed at her now-bared breasts. Heat coursed through her body. As addled as her mind had become, she couldn't tell if the warmth was due to embarrassment or a wave of desire triggered by the look on his face.

"Beautiful," he murmured just before he took one pebbled nipple into his mouth.

Her breath caught in her throat.

He suckled and teased first one breast then the other. Moisture pooled between her legs and she grew restless with need. By the time he finished and returned his attentions to her mouth she was desperate for his kiss.

When he stopped long enough to unhook her bra, she had the presence of mind to tug Randy's shirt off. His bare skin pressed against hers felt like heaven itself, but was still not enough. For either of them, it seemed.

"Wrap your legs around my waist," Randy demanded between kisses.

Nicki complied.

He carried her from the kitchen to the couch in the den without breaking their kiss. When he laid her back, she gloried in the feel of his body pressed against hers.

Between kisses she realized he'd managed to unbutton and

unzip her jeans but struggled to slip them off. With her legs still wrapped around Randy's hips, he would never manage it. She adjusted her position and helped him slide the denim down her legs.

Once more his gaze raked her all-but-naked body. She still wore her socks, but that didn't count.

He trailed kisses down her belly until he reached the juncture between her thighs. Holding her breath, she waited to see what he would do. The wicked thing held her gaze as he sat back and alternated between kisses, licks, and nips down her leg then back up. He repeated the same attention to the other leg, avoiding the one place that quivered with need.

After blazing a trail back up to her breasts and lavishing more attention there, he surprised her by settling on the floor beside the couch. Then he grasped her hips and pulled her up so he could bury his face between her legs.

She screamed out his name in shock and ecstasy. Her world spun out of control. She became nothing but sensation. Before long she reached the pinnacle and fell over the cliff into sheer bliss.

When the world righted itself, Nicki found Randy kneeling beside the couch, stroking her breasts and pressing kisses against her stomach.

She reached for him and pulled him onto the couch with her so his body covered hers. His jeans scraped against her hypersensitive skin, creating new sensations. Even after that mind-blowing orgasm, she wanted more. She wanted to feel his skin on hers.

All over.

Now.

She reached between them and found the closure on his jeans. He had to lift some of his weight off so she could open them completely. When she started to slide the jeans out of the way, he stopped her.

"Nicki, you're going to have to stop for a minute."

"What? Why?" She blinked, not understanding.

"Are you on the pill?"

"Huh? Oh." Nicki flushed from head to toe. She had been so lost in the moment she hadn't even thought of protection. "No, I, uh…" Seeing no point in dancing around the subject she blurted out the truth. "I haven't been with anyone in quite a while so, no."

When she found the courage to look up at Randy's face, his

expression said her answer had pleased him.

"I don't suppose you have any condoms with you, do you?" she asked, hoping to redirect his focus.

"I should have a couple in my shaving kit."

His answer both relieved and worried her. As far as her hormones were concerned, it was a good thing he had them. She'd worry about why he brought them later. Much later.

"However…" Randy paused. "My shaving kit is in the bathroom." He held her gaze as he added, "All the way at the other end of the cabin."

Nicki smiled, seeing no problem with changing locations. "I guess that will give us about, what? Twenty yards to, uh, work back up to it?"

Randy scooped Nicki in his arms and took off for the back bedroom, making her squeal in surprise. "Who needs to work back up to anything? I'm still ready to go."

CHAPTER TWENTY

Randy lay on the bed with one arm folded behind his head, the other wrapped around Nicki as he listened to the sound of tree branches crackling outside the cabin. There would be a lot of debris to clean up after the ice brought down the weaker limbs of the surrounding trees.

For now he wanted to soak up the feeling of Nicki curled up next him.

He didn't expect to end up in bed with her this weekend. Even in his wildest dreams he would have guessed he had months of wooing in front of him to get to that point. Now that he had, he planned to use it to his advantage. Whatever it took to win her back.

Nicki was meant for him. He just had to make her believe it as well.

A musical ringtone echoed down the hallway, causing her to stir. If memory served him correctly, it was one of the songs from *Victor Victoria*. But Nicki didn't seem to be any more inclined to move from the warmth of the bed than him.

"I suppose I should get up and answer that," she mumbled against the side of his chest.

"You can call them back, whoever it is."

"It's Steve."

Randy tensed then remembered she had said Steve was like a brother to her. "Does he know where you are?"

"Yeah."

He ran his free hand across her ribs. "You can call him back later."

"I haven't talked to him since I first got here."

Despite her protest, she still didn't try to get up. That pleased him more than it should have.

"He worries as much as Nana and will just keep calling until he gets through."

Randy rolled and pinned her to the bed beneath him. "I think we should just stay here until the ice melts."

Her smile made his heart flip in his chest.

"As marvelous as that idea sounds, we'll need to eat and take a shower sometime soon."

He nuzzled her neck. "Showering together would be good. Let's go."

Nicki laughed and swatted his left butt cheek. "Yeah, right. I've got a treasure chest to open."

He lifted his head and grinned. "Keep that up and we'll see who ends up with all the booty."

"Besides, you only have one more condom, right?"

Randy went back to nuzzling Nicki's neck, hoping to distract her from the idea of getting out of bed. "Yeah, but there are all kinds of other things we can do that don't require one. And if I get desperate, I'm pretty sure Pop has a pair of snowshoes out in the barn I can use to hike to the general store."

Nicki's laughter was music to his ears. It meant that, at least for the moment, she had relaxed with him. In retaliation for the swat on the fanny he'd received, Randy looked for the spots on both sides of her waist he remembered being ticklish.

Before long they had kicked all the covers and most of the pillows off the bed and were wrestling over who tickled who.

Out of breath from laughing, Nicki conceded. "You win. You're bigger and stronger than me."

"Yeah, but you squirm a lot and you're sneakier."

"Gordon and Billy taught me a few tricks over the years. You're lucky I didn't try any of the self-defense moves they taught me."

"So when you almost kneed me in the nuts, it wasn't deliberate?"

"No, I really didn't mean to." She leaned over, bringing them face-to-face. "How can I make it up to you?"

The suggestive tone in her voice caught the attention of more than one part of his body. "Will you kiss them and make them better?"

"Certainly." She added, "But not until later."

Randy let out an exaggerated sigh. "Okay, fine." He reached up a tweaked one of her still-bare breasts. "Later."

Before he could think of another way to distract her, Nicki sprang out of bed and ran to the bathroom. The door closing behind her told him she probably wanted a bit of privacy. When he heard the shower kick on, he forced himself to *not* join her.

Instead he busied himself by tossing the sheet and blankets back on the bed in a somewhat neat fashion. After all, there was little point in making up the bed. If he had any say in the matter, Nicki would be sleeping with him. He didn't much care which bed they used as long as she lay next to him.

Preferably naked.

Then again, they could camp out on the floor of the den like they used to. He rolled the idea around in his head, debating whether or not the old memories would help his cause or hurt it.

Better play it by ear. After all, they had tonight and maybe even tomorrow night before Nicki could even attempt to leave, given the amount of ice on the roads.

The water in the shower shut off and the other door to the bathroom opened and closed. Images of Nicki tiptoeing from the bathroom to the other bedroom in little more than a damp towel flitted through his mind's eye. Before he chased her down like an animal in heat, he grabbed some clean clothes and headed to the bathroom.

Unconcerned with privacy, he left both doors open. If she wanted a peep show, he didn't mind providing it. Hell, if she wanted to join him, she'd be welcomed with open arms. Just as he turned on the shower he heard Nicki's phone ring again. The same ring tone he'd heard earlier.

He tried to not eavesdrop, but her voice carried through the open doors. "Hey, Steve." There was a pause. "I'm fine, but I think we're going to be stuck for another day or two. We still haven't been able to get the tree off my car." Another pause. "Yeah, he's still here, too." Randy knew it was wrong, but now that he knew she was talking about him, it was hard to not listen. "No, I haven't told him."

His hand hovered in the air over the towel he had been reaching for. Told him what?

"I know. You said that. And I promise, I'll tell him, but it doesn't change anything."

He slowly pulled the towel from the closet and listened harder.

"That's true. Okay, okay, okay. Yeah, I know." Her voice trailed off.

He stepped into the bedroom in time to see her heading toward the den with the phone still pressed against her ear.

He frowned and stepped back into the bathroom. What in the world would she need to tell him that Steve would know about? They hadn't seen each other or talked in almost eight years. She said she didn't have a boyfriend, so that wasn't it.

Unless she'd lied.

No. She had no reason to lie to him about that. As skittish as she'd been about being close to him, a boyfriend would have been the perfect excuse to keep him at arm's length.

Randy got into the shower as he turned ideas and scenarios around in his head, trying to solve the puzzle. His thoughts were still churning even after he finished shaving. He pulled on clean clothes and went to look for Nicki. He found her sitting in the middle of the floor of the den with the chest in front of her. There were a few trinkets and tiny figurines scattered around her.

He stifled his impulse to demand to know what she had been talking about and settled for something less confrontational. "Did you find what you were looking for?"

Without taking her eyes off whatever she held, she said, "I think so."

He sat on the edge of the couch so he could see what had captivated her. She held a small painting, about the size of a quarter sheet of paper. From where he sat, it appeared to be a landscape. It was blurry, as if the artist had been looking through an out-of-focus lens. He'd seen similar paintings in museums, but couldn't recall any of the artists or what the style had been called. Based on the way Nicki stared at it, the painting must be a good find.

"And?" he prompted.

When she finally looked up she wore a dazed expression. "I think this may be a Monet."

CHAPTER TWENTY-ONE

"Damn. I wish I had brought my laptop," Nicole muttered as she stared at the painting in her lap. "I'm dying to do some research."

"Were you serious about it being a Monet?" Randy asked from behind her.

She couldn't suppress the shiver of awareness that ran through her when Randy leaned over her shoulder and looked at the painting.

"Yes, but I'm not one hundred percent certain. I don't remember Monet doing anything this small. Particularly during the time period this would have been purchased." She racked her brain for everything she knew about the artist. "But that doesn't mean that one of his full-size paintings didn't get cut into several smaller ones."

He scooted off the couch and sat on the floor next to her. "Why would someone cut up a famous artist's painting?"

She shrugged. "You never know what people will do for money. A Monet is still a Monet."

"Seems a shame to destroy someone's work like that."

The sincerity on his face touched her. Pleased that he felt the same way she did, she kissed him softly on the lips.

"Not that I'm complaining, but that was a very sweet kiss. What was it for?"

"I dunno. I just felt like it."

He wrapped his arm around her waist and pulled her closer. "Are you going to feel like it again?"

"Maybe."

Randy placed a tender kiss on her lips. One that held a promise of something more. She melted as he deepened it.

Randy's softer, loving side was just one more thing about him she missed.

Loving?

She must be mistaken. Randy didn't love her. They hadn't seen each other in years! It must be her own foolish heart hoping for more than was actually there.

This time she had to make sure her heart didn't get in the way. That annoying organ could just sit back and shut up while the rest of her body enjoyed the ride.

"You okay?" Randy asked.

She blinked away her thoughts and refocused on Randy. "Yeah. Why do you ask?"

"You tensed up as if something were wrong."

"Sorry. I had a stray thought, but it's fine." She turned her attention to the painting in her lap. "I should do something with this before it gets messed up."

"There are probably some plastic bags in the kitchen it would fit in."

Nicki shuddered in horror. "God, no. That's one of the worst things to store it in. Do you think Rosie would mind if I borrowed an old pillowcase?"

"Gram wouldn't care if you took everything you wanted out of here just because it was you. But if she knew you were taking it to protect a masterpiece, she'd probably demand you use the good pillowcases."

"I don't know for sure that it *is* a masterpiece yet. It could be something painted by one of Monet's students."

"Wouldn't that be obvious, though? Especially for someone like you?"

"Like me?"

"Yeah." He waved at the painting. "You're the expert in this stuff."

Pleased he thought her an expert, she smiled. "I'm not an expert. I've just studied a lot of art and the history behind much of it. It fascinates me."

"See? You'd know if it were a Monet or not."

"Not necessarily. If he had a student who worked with him for years and mastered his techniques, it would be hard to tell. There are also a few counterfeiters who have managed to perfect certain masters' works." She leaned the painting against the couch nearby but out of the way. "That's why I'm dying to get to my books and my computer. I want to look up a few things."

"I brought my laptop with me, but there's no Wi-Fi out here."

"I guess you don't have a hot spot on your phone either, huh?"

Randy shook his head. "Haven't needed one before. There's no shortage of them in Chicago. And even when we visit clients, it hasn't been an issue."

"Yeah, same here. But it's killing me to not be able to look up a few things."

"Just search on your phone."

"I don't know the web addresses of the sites I want to get to. I have those saved in my favorites on my computer. And a couple of them are university sites. I don't think I can get to those on my phone."

"You do realize it may be another day or two before the roads are anything close to being drivable, right?"

"Yeah. I know." She frowned. "But that's also assuming my car is okay."

He put his arm around her shoulder and squeezed. "It's probably fine."

"I hope so. I just paid it off."

Randy cringed. "Ouch. Tell you what. If the sun comes out, it should warm up enough to where we could start cutting branches. That tree is going to have to be moved before either of us can get out of the drive."

"I could use some sunshine and exercise."

He leaned closer and lowered his tone of voice, making it far more intimate. "I'd be happy to give you another," his eyebrows waggled up and down playfully, "workout."

Nicki laughed and swatted him on the arm. "You have a couple more days and nights to survive. You'd better save that other condom until you really need it."

"I already said I would dig out Pop's snowshoes and hike up to the gas station to get more. Offer still stands."

"You don't even know if they're open."

"I don't mind a little breaking and entering for that. I'd leave the money on the counter so it wouldn't be stealing."

From his expression, Nicki couldn't be sure if he was serious or not. "You are bad."

Randy reached over and threaded his fingers into her hair then pulled her closer. "That's what you do to me, Nicki."

He captured her lips in a heated kiss. In a heartbeat her body responded. She leaned closer, craving more. Even after their very thorough and very satisfying encounter earlier, she still wanted him. Before she realized what she was doing she had crawled into his lap and straddled him. All without breaking their kiss.

His hands caressed her up and down her back and her hips. Given the sizable lump in his jeans, she affected him as much as he did her. Before things went too far and they forgot about anything except each other, Nicki eased out of their kiss. She forced herself to meet his gaze, to look for clues to what he might be feeling. Beyond his obvious physical response, anyway.

She needed to be careful to not get in too deep where he was concerned.

His eyes met hers and held. Instinctively she knew he had opened himself to her scrutiny. Letting her see what he felt inside. The thought both alarmed and fascinated her. Did she dare look? What if she didn't like what she found?

She didn't know what she wanted right now, so what good would answers about his feelings do her? She could file the thought away for later. When she could think clearly. When the smell and feel of Randy didn't affect her and make her want things that were not there.

Taking the easy way out, Nicki looked down to where their hips were separated by a couple pieces of denim. "I, uh… Sorry." She blushed. "I got carried away."

"If that's how you get carried away, feel free to do it anytime with me."

Embarrassed by her immediate and overpowering reaction to Randy's kiss, she looked for something else to focus on. "I should finish going through the chest so we can put it away."

Randy didn't seem to be in a big hurry to move her off his lap. Instead of rubbing her back, he caressed her waist and her thighs and asked, "What else did you find in there, other than the painting?"

His touch made it hard to focus on anything, but she managed to gather a few brain cells to respond. "A few mementos and a couple of pictures. I haven't opened the last two drawers yet, though."

Liana Garson

"Curiosity was always your weakness. Why haven't you gotten into them yet?"

She lifted her chin. "I got a little distracted."

"Really?" He pretended innocence. "By what?"

"A Monet, for one thing," she said, still straddling his lap.

"Anything else?"

"Oh, I dunno, something else might have popped up and sidetracked me." She ground her pelvis against his erection.

He growled. "Careful."

Appeased by his reaction, she suggested, "Come on. Let's see what else is in that chest."

106

CHAPTER TWENTY-TWO

It was taking a healthy dose of control to not ask Nicki about the phone conversation he'd overheard while in the bathroom. Her excitement over the painting was contagious and he didn't want to distract her just yet. His gut warned him that whatever she needed to tell him wasn't going to make him very happy.

He picked up the letters Nicki had stacked next to the chest and looked at the postmarks. They were addressed to Charlotte Taylor. Nicki's grandmother. Taylor must have been her maiden name. The letters had postmarks that spanned a little over six months during 1951.

Would it be intruding on Charlotte's privacy to read them?

He'd ask Nicki when she got off the phone with her boss. She might have already read them, but he doubted it. She'd been too consumed with the second painting she'd found in the bottom drawer of the chest to do much else. Like the first one, she didn't know for certain who had painted it but doubted it was another Monet.

Her excitement over the finds made her vibrate with energy. But the idea of her telling anyone about the paintings made him uncomfortable. Right now she could only think of bringing a new masterpiece into the art community, but her own safety needed to be considered. If word got out to the wrong people, it might place her in danger until the paintings could be secured someplace appropriate.

A Monet would be worth a lot of money, maybe even millions. People did stupid things for money.

He hoped like hell her boss realized the possible danger to Nicki before he advertised the find on the news and drew unwanted attention her way. From her side of their phone conversation, her boss must be reluctant to believe she had found something that valuable. Nicki had to repeat several times that, yes, it appeared to be a Monet, but she would have to do some research to confirm that.

The knot in his chest eased somewhat when she told her boss she didn't want anything said about it on the news. Sadly her reluctance to say anything to the public came from her need to confirm the painting's origin rather than her safety.

Randy turned his attention to the letters and trinkets scattered on the floor around the chest as Nicki ended her call.

"I don't think he believed me," Nicki said with some amusement as she flopped into the nearby the chair.

"Why do you think that?"

"I had to repeat 'Monet' to him several times. I think he thought I was pulling his leg or something."

"Did you tell him you were stuck here for a couple more days?"

"Yeah, I did. He said they would cover for me if I couldn't get back by Monday morning."

"Good. There's no point in rushing out of here just because of a painting. Even if it is a Monet, it's been stashed away for fifty years. It won't hurt to keep it hidden for a few more days."

"I know, I know. I'm just anxious to look up some information about both of the paintings so I can find out for sure who created them."

"Have you called Charlotte yet?"

"I called her before I called Bob."

Because he couldn't not touch her, he pulled Nicki into his lap. "Was she surprised?"

Her brow furrowed. "Actually, no. She didn't know who the artist was, but she remembered her mother being very protective of those paintings. It wasn't until she went to an art exhibit in St. Louis that she understood why. Some of the paintings she saw were similar enough to make her wonder if her mother's had been done by someone important."

Nicki snuggled into his lap without protest. He doubted she even realized her instinct was to touch him back when she played with the buttons on his flannel shirt. "Why didn't she try to find out before now?"

"Nana said she figured the paintings would be better off tucked away. Kind of like a rainy-day security blanket. Then after a while, she didn't think about them again."

Randy grunted in response as he stroked Nicki's back.

"She said the only reason they did pop into her head again was because she went looking for some old letters. When she recalled storing the letters in the chest, she remembered the paintings."

"And with you being an art expert and all, she thought you might be interested in the paintings?"

"Uh-huh." Nicki closed her eyes and laid her head on his shoulder as he ran his fingers up her back and into her hair.

She had pulled her hair back and secured it in one of those stretchy things, but he tugged it loose so he could run his fingers through the long reddish-brown strands.

It was hard to control himself with her being so receptive to his attentions. He wanted nothing more than to touch her, to see how many different ways he could make her sigh with pleasure or moan with ecstasy. He could spend a lifetime finding out. She didn't know it yet, but that was exactly what he planned to do.

He needed to make her understand he wanted more than just a weekend romp.

"Did Charlotte say where the letters came from?"

"Hhhmmm?" Nicki sounded drowsy snuggled against him.

Randy smiled. She was well on her way to being boneless. He liked knowing he could do that to her. "The letters Charlotte wanted?" he prompted.

"What about them?" she mumbled.

"Are those the letters there? Next to the chest?"

Nicki turned her head and looked in the direction of the chest. "Yeah, I think so."

"Did you read them?" he asked as he continued to rub her neck.

"No. I wasn't sure I should."

"She didn't say who they were from?"

Nicki shook her head against his neck. "No."

Randy rested his chin on top of her head and ran his fingers down the silky strands of her hair. The clean smell of Nicki's shampoo teased his senses. "Aren't you curious?" He smiled to himself, already knowing her answer.

Her hand slipped inside his flannel shirt and she caressed his chest and shoulder as she snuggled closer, making him almost forget he'd even asked her a question.

"A little," she answered.

He tugged on her hair until she looked up at him. Her eyes were soft and filed with curiosity. Holding her gaze, he kissed her. Not a passion-fueled kiss but a gentle one that he hoped conveyed what he felt since he had no words.

She sighed against his lips. Even if her brain didn't get his message, some part of her understood.

Without breaking their kiss, he shifted position until he lay on the floor with Nicki draped across him. Despite the cool, hardwood floor beneath him, he was comfortable. Nicki didn't seem to mind either.

The lazy kisses turned playful as each of them tried to goad the other into a bigger smile or laugh. They wrestled and tickled and explored each other's bodies until they were both breathless. Randy started to demand Nicki's unconditional surrender when her cell phone rang.

She searched through the pillows scattered on the floor until she found her phone. Her forehead creased into a frown when she looked at the caller ID.

"What's wrong?" he asked.

"It's Ed. I don't know why he'd be calling."

Who the hell was Ed? With a grumble he said, "Only one way to find out."

Nicki nodded her agreement and clicked the button to answer.

Trying not to eavesdrop, Randy picked up a couple of pillows and tossed them back onto the couch then went to build up the fire again. Whoever Ed was, Nicki didn't look pleased to hear from him. Despite his initial reaction, there didn't seem to be any point in being jealous.

Nicki ended her conversation and set her phone down next to the chest in the center of the room. Shaking her head, she told him, "You know, sometimes I just don't get him."

"What do you mean?" Randy pushed the new log into place on the fire with the poker.

"I went out with him one time. It wasn't even a real date. We attended the same gallery opening on behalf of the station. But ever since then he acts as if he can butt into my business whenever the mood strikes him."

Randy stopped stoking the fire so he could see Nicki's reaction.

"What did he say?"

She folded her arms across her chest. "He wanted to know where I was and when I'd be back."

"I assume you told him it was none of his business."

"Sort of. I told him the same thing I told him before I left. I was out of town and I'd be back in a couple more days."

Randy frowned. "Didn't you say he works at the station?"

"Yeah, why?"

"Did he ask about the paintings?"

"No, why?"

He turned back to the fire before answering. "Just wondering if your boss might have said something to him about the Monet."

"Doubtful. Bob tolerates Ed, but I have never gotten the sense that he likes him. I seriously doubt he'd confide in Ed. Especially since I asked Bob not to say anything yet."

Somewhat comforted, Randy let the subject drop. Besides, there were more important things to focus on right now. Like finding the most sensitive spot on Nicki's body.

He set the fire poker on the rack. "All right, woman." Randy placed his fists on his hips and puffed out his chest. "Since you were forced to surrender early due to an untimely interruption, I've decided to be gracious and allow you a rematch."

"Reeeaaaallly," Nicki drawled. "And if I don't recall surrendering?"

He took two steps toward Nicki, his intent written clearly across his face. "Then the game is still on."

She shrieked and sprinted toward the bedrooms.

Randy smiled and gave chase.

CHAPTER TWENTY-THREE

Randy stared up at the ceiling as he and Nicki recovered from their wrestling match. Even though he knew she wouldn't appreciate the fact that he'd eavesdropped on her phone conversation, he didn't want to put off his questions any longer.

"There's something I've been wanting to ask you."

"What's that?" she murmured against the side of his chest as her finger drew tiny circles on his belly.

"I overhead you talking on the phone with Steve yesterday." She stiffened. "I was about to get into the shower, but when I went to get a towel, your voice came through loud and clear."

"What exactly did you hear?"

"You told Steve that you were planning to tell me something, you just didn't know what difference it would make."

Her finger stopped moving.

"Is there something I need to know about?"

"I, uh…" She rolled onto her back and looked up at the ceiling.

"Nicki." He rolled to his side and looked at her. "Whatever it is, just tell me. I suspect I've thought of ten things far worse than whatever you need to say."

She sat up and clutched the sheet to her chest. "I doubt that."

"You said you don't have a boyfriend, right?"

She shook her head in the negative.

"A fiancé?"

"No."

The breath he didn't realize he'd been holding eased. "Do you have an STD?"

She frowned at him. "Good God, no."

"Well, then, what? I'm just guessing here. But everything else I come up with is uphill from there."

"I don't know that it matters."

"Steve knows about it, though, right?"

She nodded and bit her lip. Even from his angle he could see that her eyes had become teary.

"If you could tell him, why can't you tell me?"

"Because it had nothing to do with him."

His chest tightened. Images of Nicki being attacked late at night bombarded his mind's eye. He clamped down on that train of thought as he started seeing red. "Who does it have to do with?"

She turned and looked at him. "You."

His brain seized. "Me?" He sat up in bed. "Well, if it has something to do with me, don't you think you should tell me?"

"It was eight years ago. There's nothing you can do about it now."

Randy's brain sprang to life and attempted to grasp new ideas about what she was keeping from him, but it kept coming up empty. "Now I'm really confused. What are you talking about?"

"Steve thinks you have a right to know about the baby."

He blinked, hoping to jump start his thoughts. "Baby?"

Nicki looked at him. "I was pregnant when you left eight years ago."

He wanted to deny what she was saying but, based on the pain he saw in her eyes, knew he couldn't. "What happened?"

She pulled her knees up to her chest beneath the sheet and wrapped her arms around them. "After you left I tried to call you, almost daily, trying to find out why you left. Why you were suddenly no longer speaking to me. Eventually I quit trying. I figured if you wanted to talk to me, you'd call."

Randy grimaced, remembering how much of an ass he'd been.

"A couple weeks later, I missed my period. I chalked it up to stress. But when I missed the second one, I just knew. I took a home pregnancy test and sure enough, I was pregnant." She grasped her toes through the sheet. "Steve went with me to get checked. The doctor confirmed the results and calculated a due date for me. Steve held my hand all the way home."

"Why didn't you tell me?"

"I tried." She gave him a tight-lipped smile. "That night when I got home from the doctor, I called you. Your mom answered and said you were out with friends. She was supposed to give you a message to please call me." She shook her head. "But you never did."

"Dammit." Guilt flooded his system.

"About a week later I miscarried."

Randy shoved one hand into his hair. He closed his eyes and silently berated himself for being one of the lowest sons of bitches on the planet.

"Thankfully I was back at college by then, so Mom never found out."

He finally looked at her. "Shit, Nicki. I'm sorry."

She shrugged. "Like I said, it was eight years ago. There's nothing either of us can do to change what happened."

"Yeah, but I was an idiot and treated you like shit. And then you had to deal with that on top of it?" He shook his head. "That's too much."

She gave him a half grin. "I thought so too at the time. But Steve got me through it. He made sure I went to my classes so I didn't sit around feeling sorry for myself. I couldn't have gotten through it without him."

"No wonder you two are so close," he murmured. "Did the doctor say what happened? *Why* it happened?" He couldn't bring himself to say baby. It was just too much for him to take in.

She shook her head. "No. It was just one of those things."

"You haven't had any problems since?"

She gave him a strange look. "If you mean any other pregnancies, no."

He waved his hand toward her abdomen. "No, I mean, is everything working fine now?"

"Oh, yeah. My doctor assured me everything is fine. I should be able to have kids if and when I'm ready."

He nodded. "Good. I, uh… Yeah. Good."

"Look, Randy, I know this is a bit of a shock to you. I honestly debated whether or not I should tell you. I mean, after all, it's been eight years. Quite frankly, if you never found out, it wouldn't change anything. But Steve felt strongly that you should know."

"No. Yeah. I'm, uh…" He ran his hand through his hair again. "I'm glad you told me. I just hate it that you had to go through that."

"Not trying to make you feel any guiltier than you probably do, but believe me, the emotional loss was far worse than the physical, so don't make it into a bigger deal than it was."

He reached for her and pulled her into his embrace. "God, I'm sorry, Nicki."

She laid her head on his shoulder and wrapped her arms around his chest. "It took a while, but I've come to terms with it. It just wasn't meant to be and it was probably for the best. We weren't ready to be parents."

"Maybe we weren't, but I still hate it that you had to go through that."

"Thank you."

Her ability to forgive was humbling. Some women would have ranted and raved, thrown things, and called him all kinds of hateful names. But not his Nicki.

She really was one of a kind.

The kind you treated like a queen and worshiped daily.

Somehow he had to make it up to her. He just needed a plan for getting her back into his life.

CHAPTER TWENTY-FOUR

Nicki stretched her pleasantly sore muscles then snuggled up against Randy. She'd forgotten how much she enjoyed waking up next to a warm, male body. Despite the layers of ice and snow outside, she was nice and toasty. Even without clothes.

She smiled as she recalled the number of ways she and Randy made each other come without actually having intercourse. After all, they were saving that last condom until they just couldn't stand it any longer.

If last night was any indication, tonight would be the limit on that condom. They'd wrestled and tickled until she'd finally conceded defeat.

Even their emotional detour when she told him about her miscarriage hadn't dampened their desire for each other. If anything, it added another layer of intimacy by forcing them to talk through some things.

He seemed to genuinely regret what he'd done.

And based on his actions afterward, he seemed determined to replace those memories with new ones. Him trying to teach her how to decipher the letters he drew with his tongue as he licked her most private spot would be something she wouldn't forget anytime soon.

Even though he hadn't made it past four letters before she got lost in a fog of sensation.

After he made her orgasm at least three more times, they ate sandwiches in bed, then she returned the favor and made his eyes roll back in his head.

She could get used to being held throughout the night. And fast.

Oh man.

Nicki studied Randy. His eyes were closed and his breathing remained slow and shallow.

What would have happened to them if he hadn't run off to Chicago? Or at least, if he had been up front with her about what had been going on in his life? What if she had never had a broken heart? Would they have lasted all this time?

Or had they been too young with too much time and too many life lessons ahead of them?

Perhaps fate had given them this weekend in order to have a chance to make their relationship work after all.

Afraid of where her thoughts were taking her, Nicki slipped carefully from the bed and headed to the bathroom. As she brushed her teeth and washed her face, she couldn't dismiss the idea that a power greater than either of them wanted them together. That maybe it was meant to be.

She stepped into the shower, reminding herself that being with Randy meant she would have to let down the wall she'd built around her heart and open herself up to the possibility of getting hurt again. She wasn't sure she could. She'd gotten good at hiding behind that wall. It was safe. It was comfortable.

Besides, all of that assumed that Randy wanted more than just a weekend fling. Nothing he'd said or done indicated he did.

Enough with the foolishness!

She should just enjoy the weekend then return to Springfield relaxed enough to be able to refocus on her job.

As she stepped out of the shower, she told herself that was what was important.

She exited the bathroom to the bedroom where her things were and found a change of clothes. After pulling on her last pair of clean jeans, she went to the kitchen.

While she waited for the coffeepot to work its magic, she stared at the winter wonderland out the kitchen window. The sun had just come up and made sparkles in the ice crystals that coated everything around the cabin. Part of her wanted to grab a coat and run out to play in it. She wanted to make snow angels, stomp her feet on the ground and listen to the ice crunch, and maybe even shake the ice from a tree just to watch it rain down.

The adult part of her said, maybe later, after breakfast.

A noise in the den caught her attention. She turned and found

Randy striding into the kitchen wearing nothing but a pair of plaid flannel pants. His hair was still in disarray, but his eyes were alert and focused on her.

The sight of his bare chest and abs started a flutter in her belly.

"Good morning." He had that husky just-woke-up voice that made her question why she'd even gotten out of bed.

"Good morning."

He pinned her against the counter and nuzzled her neck. "Is that coffee I smell?"

Her knees turned to jelly. "I would hope it's my soap you're smelling right now."

He stopped nuzzling her neck and looked down at her with a grin. "You have soap that smells like coffee? No wonder the men are throwing themselves at you."

Nicki swatted his shoulder. "And all this time I thought men just liked my boobs."

Still keeping his hold on her waist, Randy pulled back and looked down at her chest. "They are very nice boobs." He leaned down and placed a kiss on the top of each. "I'm quite fond of them."

"Glad to know it," she mumbled.

Still grinning, he asked, "What are you doing up so early? I had hoped you'd want to stay in bed all morning."

"One of us had to make coffee. It wouldn't have been pretty without it."

"Probably true," he agreed.

"And we have things to do today."

"You bed, er, I mean, you bet we do." Randy wagged his eyebrows suggestively.

"Uh-huh." Nicki nudged him aside so she could get to the coffeepot. She filled two mugs with the steaming java. "We have a tree to move off my car."

He took the offered mug. "I suppose we could work that in today."

Nicki grunted in response.

"And since we have electricity, you're probably going to want me to cook, too, huh?"

"If you want something other than cold sandwiches, you might want to at least help." She took a sip from her mug. "What else did you find in the freezer? Anything we could just pop in the oven and heat up?"

"Maybe." Randy looked in the direction of the back porch, where the deep freeze stood. "I saw a couple of casserole dishes, but I'm not sure what's in them."

"I hate to make work for Rosie. She fixed all that stuff for the party. If we keep getting into it, she'll have to make more."

Randy shrugged one shoulder. "She and Pop said for us to help ourselves. It will be several weeks before they can reschedule the party. That's assuming they can find another weekend that everyone is free."

"I still feel bad about it."

"Will it make you feel better if I told you that I'd already thought about hiring a caterer to make it up to them?"

"A little," she admitted.

"Then it's settled. We'll raid the freezer and not feel bad about it." He lifted one eyebrow. "Agreed?"

"Agreed."

Randy dropped a playful kiss on her mouth. "Good. Now quit worrying about the little things and focus on the big ones. We've got a tree to move."

Nicki nodded. "Yeah." *And a heart to keep in line.*

They finished breakfast then dressed to go outside and work on the tree. Although the dressing part took longer than expected, since they both had trouble keeping their hands to themselves. At one point she contemplated a new way to use her scarf. One that didn't involve being outside in the cold.

But eventually they made it to the barn to collect the tools they'd need then, finally, the car.

"How do you suppose we should tackle it?" she asked.

"Why don't you use the clippers and see how many of those smaller branches you can clear away while I start working on the trunk with the chain saw. I'd like to cut as much weight as we can so we don't have to scrape the top any more than we'll have to when we pull it off."

Images of Randy slipping on the ice with a running chain saw ran through her mind and made her cringe. "Be careful with that thing."

He winked. "I will."

They both went to work and made more progress than she expected in such a short amount of time. When Randy called for a

119

break and demanded she go in and warm up, they could see most of the car.

The tree had left a sizeable dent in the hood, but Randy had been correct with his initial assessment. It didn't look as though the engine or tires had been damaged. That meant she should be able to drive home as soon as the roads were clear.

But going home meant their time together was almost over. That she might not see Randy again for another eight years. If ever again.

Her heart squeezed.

Damn. This weekend was supposed to be about sex and letting go of old hurts. She meant to keep her foolish heart under lock and key. What happened to her plan?

"Hey. You okay?" Randy asked.

"Yeah." She forced a smile. "I believe you said something about hot chocolate and a fire?"

He frowned. "I did, but there for a minute you looked as if you wanted to be anyplace but here. What's wrong?"

"Nothing. Sorry. I was just thinking about the things I needed to do as soon as I get back to the office."

"Are you sure that's all that's bothering you?"

"The idea of an expensive repair bill isn't sitting well with me," she lied.

"I understand that. Especially if you just paid it off."

She turned away with a groan. "Don't remind me." When she reached the porch she asked, "You want me to just leave the clippers here?"

He pointed to the door. "Up there, out of the snow. I'll put them away after we're finished with them."

"Are you coming in?" As much as she couldn't afford to get any closer, she didn't want to waste any of the time they had left together. And when he touched her she didn't have the ability to think about what would come later. "I was thinking we could play a round of 'hide the marshmallow' to warm up."

"Well, I'm certainly not missing out on that." He grabbed the chain saw and rushed up the stairs as fast as the ice would let him. With a thud, he dropped the tools on the porch and hustled her through the door. "Come on! What are you waiting for?" He swatted her on the fanny, making her squeal in surprise. "I've got marshmallows to find!"

CHAPTER TWENTY-FIVE

The rest of the day they alternated between cleaning away the tree and reveling in each other's bodies. By the time the sun went down, they were pleasantly exhausted. They snuggled on the couch and halfway watched a TV show Nicki claimed to be one of her favorites. But he had no trouble redirecting her attention from the program.

When the news came on neither of them were surprised to see the weather as the headline. A bundled-up reporter standing near a highway informed them all major roads were now passable thanks to the efforts of the local road crews. Yet the highway patrol still encouraged people to remain indoors unless travel was absolutely necessary.

His time with Nicki was drawing to a close. But he had no sense of whether or not he'd made progress with her. Yes, her body responded to him, but had she forgiven him for leaving?

"How about if I run a bath for us?"

"A bath? For both of us?"

"After working that chain saw and doing all that lifting, I could use a good soak. What about you?"

She shrugged. "I'm a little sore but not bad."

"Come on. It'll be good for you." He nuzzled her ear and whispered, "I'll rub all your tender spots while we're in there."

She grinned. "That I won't turn down."

He urged her to sit up. "I'll go turn the heater on in the bathroom and start the water. Why don't you grab a bottle of wine and a couple of glasses?"

"All right."

He still saw some reluctance in her eyes. As if she held back and wanted to keep him at arm's length. Even though he understood it, he hated it.

He got up and headed to the master bathroom before she saw his frustration and confused it for something else. What did he expect? They'd been thrown together for a few days. He had no right to think that had been enough time to overcome years of hurt and distance.

For some reason the lights in the bathroom seemed bright and harsh. He found a few candles in the corner and lit all of them with the pack of matches that had been tucked behind the largest. When he was sure the flames would stay lit, he turned off the overhead lights. Candlelight was supposed to be romantic, right?

He flipped the switch on the built-in heater then turned on the hot water to the tub. Before he could finish going through the bath products on the edge of the tub, Nicki came in.

"Oh good. How about if I take those," he reached for the wine and glasses she held, "and you pick one of these?" He nodded to the soap stuff he had just been looking through.

She smiled and handed him the items. "Okay."

He set the wine and glasses on the floor next to the tub then checked the temperature of the water. Nicki added a little of the powdered stuff from one of the jars, sending a sweet vanilla scent into the air.

When she turned to face him, he pulled her into his arms.

Holding her gaze, he slowly lowered his lips to hers. And with that lightest of touches, the smoldering flame that never seemed to go out when he was near Nicki burst into a raging inferno. It took every ounce of control to not rip her clothes off.

He eased away from their kiss and took a step back. "Before this goes any further, I need to slow down. Tonight I want to indulge you. To worship every part of your body."

Her breath hitched, and even in the dim candlelight he could tell her pupils had dilated.

"Let me start by helping you undress." He worked the buttons of her flannel shirt free then pushed the fabric over her shoulders. The sleeves caught at her wrists. Nicki raised a brow in question.

The idea of having her bound before him in a gesture of total trust held considerable appeal, but that was not what he planned. Tonight needed to be about her and making her feel everything he could offer.

He pushed the sleeves over her hands and let the fabric fall to the floor. Starting at her waist, he pushed her T-shirt up, skimming his hands over her skin as he went. When he reached her breasts, he flicked his thumbs over her nipples and made her gasp. Without stopping, he pulled the stretchy fabric over her head and let it join the other garment on the floor.

She reached for him but he stopped her hands and pushed them back down to her sides. "No. I want to do this."

She bit her lip and nodded once.

When the tub reached the half-full mark, he switched the faucet off and sat on the edge. He gestured for Nicki to step closer. When she complied he ran the tops of his knuckles over her breast. "Lovely."

The closure of her jeans was next. As soon as he unfastened the button and lowered the zipper he pushed his hands inside her waistband. Her skin was soft as the finest silk.

He pulled her closer and pressed his lips against her stomach. Without taking his mouth off, he pushed her jeans over her hips and down to her ankles. He ran his tongue around her belly button then down to the patch of hair at her juncture.

The breathless sounds she made were sexier than anything he'd ever heard.

He reached for her ankle and lifted her foot just enough to push the bunched-up fabric off then set it down and repeated it with the other foot.

Seeing her naked while he remained dressed gave him a heady sense of power. He stood then grasped her around the back of her head and pulled her toward him. He meant to keep the kiss gentle but he wanted her too damn much for that.

Her body melted against his. He ran his hand down her back, tracing her curves and relishing the way she felt.

His desire for her was quickly spinning out of control. He had to get a leash on it. This night needed to be about her to demonstrate how good they could be together, not about his needs.

He broke their kiss. "Into the tub."

She moved slow and unsteady, as if drugged. He kept one hand on her to ensure she didn't slip. The knowledge that he had that effect on her made him stand a little taller.

Once she settled in the tub, he poured a glass of wine and handed it to her. "Here."

"Aren't you going to join me?"

"Of course. I just need to get a couple of things."

He took towels and a washcloth from the linen cabinet and put them next to the tub. Then he whipped his shirt off and tossed it on the pile of Nicki's clothes.

"You know, you could go a little slower there, cowboy." She smirked at him over the rim of her glass. "Make it last, baby."

He chuckled and turned so he faced her. Drawing on the things he'd seen at the strip clubs, he ran his hand down his chest and belly to his crotch. Taking his time, he slipped the button of his jeans free. Despite having done it a hundred times before, he fumbled with the zipper. But he managed to keep his cool and lower it. Nicki seemed to be mesmerized by everything he did.

Turning his back to her, he eased his jeans and his briefs over his hips, gave her a wink over his shoulder, then bent at the waist and pushed the fabric all the way to his ankles. When he wiggled his butt, she giggled with delight.

He laughed as he freed his feet from the tangle of clothing and kicked it aside. The grin on her face was worth any embarrassment he felt during his performance.

"Lean forward so I can climb in."

She complied and he settled in behind her then pulled her against his chest as he reclined against the tub. The hot water chased the chill from his feet.

"Do you want any?" She jiggled her glass where he could see it.

"Yes, but not wine."

"Oh?" She leaned forward, pushed a stray rubber duck aside, and set the glass on the edge of the tub. Then she turned over so they were chest to chest. "Then what do you want?"

"You." He pulled her by the waist until their lips met. The wine she had been drinking still lingered on her tongue. ˙

He ran his hands down her back and gripped her butt cheeks. His erection pressed against her belly but offered little relief against the building pressure.

Shifting the way she lay against him, he pushed his hand between their bodies and searched for her clit. The catch in her breathing let him know when he found the sensitive button. Without releasing her lips, he teased the bud with his fingers. He drew circles around it, but the long, firm strokes were what elicited throaty purrs from her.

With his knee he parted her legs to widen his access. He nibbled on her lower lip then moved to her ear. "What's the most you have ever come in one session?" he whispered.

"I… I'm not sure. Not counting last night, maybe twice. Why?"

"Because I'm going to shatter that record and make you forget about any other man you've been with."

He dipped his finger into her pussy then stroked the front wall of her channel as he withdrew. Nicki's muscles quivered as if shaking off a chill. Using his thumb, he pressed against her clit then flicked back and forth over the sensitive nub.

He sought her lips once again and devoured them. His goal was simple. He wanted to overwhelm her with his presence and drown her in sensations.

Using his free hand, he massaged her back and swirled warm water over the exposed skin. He teased her tongue with his and nibbled the edges of her lips just to keep her guessing.

Her first orgasm erupted with a short cry of relief.

Before she could even catch her breath, he flipped her over and settled between her legs. He locked his lips around one of her nipples and teased the bud with his tongue. Knowing her clit would likely be sensitive, he pressed his entire palm against her pussy and rubbed her opening with the tip of his finger. When she responded to his touches he sank his middle finger into her channel and pumped it in and out. Soon she was squirming beneath him, silently asking for more.

He switched to the other breast and alternated between suckling and teasing the tip with his tongue. Like a flower opening its petals, she spread her legs farther, giving him more access to her core. With just a few more strokes, her thighs began to quiver and she stiffened beneath him.

Again he gave her no time to recover. He pushed her over that cliff once more then whispered into her ear, "Sit on the edge of the tub."

She opened her eyes and blinked in confusion.

He jostled her to get her to move. "Hop up there."

When she complied, he shifted so he could kneel between her legs. He held her gaze as he pushed her knees farther apart. Her mouth fell open and her eyes became even cloudier. With a grin, he leaned in and licked her dripping pussy from bottom to top.

A shudder racked her body.

He grasped her firmly so she couldn't slide off the edge then closed his eyes and savored her essence. His licks started out slow and easy but soon built into a ravenous hunger. He sucked her clit between his teeth and her breathing stopped. When he pressed a finger into her channel and made flicking motions across her tiny nub, she grabbed his head and bowed up with a silent scream.

Her juices flowed freely and he lapped them up like a starving man.

Since Nicki was almost boneless now, he had to help her slide back into the water so he could rinse her off. He stood and grabbed one of the towels he'd left nearby. After pushing the drain open, he lifted her from the water and had her stand on the rug next to the tub. She swayed a little when he released his hold.

He draped the towel around her shoulders then grabbed the other one and wrapped it around his waist. When he climbed out, he joined her on the rug. Lifting her chin, he looked in her eyes. Her dazed expression satisfied his ego but did nothing to ease his raging hard-on.

Every place he dried on her body, he followed with a kiss. By the time he reached her dainty feet, she seemed more clearheaded, but there was an unmistakable fire smoldering inside her.

He stole one more kiss then swept her up into his arms and carried her into the bedroom.

CHAPTER TWENTY-SIX

Nicole wanted to weep at the care and tenderness Randy showed her.

But it confused her. Maybe he acted this way with all the ladies he knew he wouldn't see again.

She shook off the thought and focused on the myriad sensations he stirred in her body. Why shouldn't she bask in his attentions? It was a temporary thing. A way to scratch an itch and banish an old dream once and for all.

With her resolve in place, she wrapped her arms around his neck and returned his kiss for everything she was worth. It wouldn't hurt to give him something to remember.

But every time she tried to take control and heat things up, he turned the tables and swamped her senses. He lingered on places that no one had bothered with before, explored all of her crevices, and licked or kissed every single part of her body. No one had ever devoted so much effort to her pleasure.

By the time he rolled the last condom in place, she wanted to weep with joy. She wanted him inside her more than she wanted her next breath.

His slow, steady strokes drew her pleasure out and pulled her even more under his spell. Even though she had already come more that she thought possible, she felt the stirrings of another climax. Randy lifted her legs and deepened his penetration. His next thrust hit the spot and set off another round of fireworks in her body.

She bowed up, then her release surged through her body, sending electrical pulses to all of her cells. She shuddered and grasped at his back, trying to pull him closer. If that were possible.

He grunted and collapsed onto her.

It took a moment, then he rolled to the side and pulled her next to him. She snuggled against his chest and snaked her arm over his ribs.

Their hearts hammered against their chests and their labored breaths came in shallow gasps.

"God, I could do that every night."

Nicki nodded. "Me, too." Her eyes popped open and she froze. Had he just said what she thought he said?

Before she could finish processing the thought, Randy let out a soft snore.

She listened to his breathing and focused on the beating of his heart and tried not to think about the things she wanted but couldn't have.

Unable to stop them, dreams she thought she'd locked away surfaced. Dreams of the two of them buying an old art deco house and renovating it together. Dreams of shopping for the perfect dress for their wedding and the look on his face when he first saw her in it. Dreams of intimate breakfasts in bed and nights under the stars, snuggled in each others' arms.

But the one that twisted her heart into knots was the dream of chasing a toddler into the backyard where Randy pushed another child in a swing.

The scene was so real she could smell the flowers blooming in the nearby garden.

She nodded off thinking about how much the little boy looked like Randy.

In the wee hours of the morning, she woke to the feel of Randy cupping her breast. Her back spooned into his front while his erection rubbed against her butt cheek. In her warm, sleepy state, she offered no protest when he pulled her leg over his, opening her up to his attentions. His talented fingers slid down her belly and into the thatch of hair at her juncture. As he rubbed her clit, he slipped inside her.

With slow, easy movements he rocked in and out of her body, drawing out their pleasure. His lips teased the ridge of her ear and the stubble on his cheek scraped against the sensitive spot on her neck. Keeping his hold on her breast, he pinched her nipple, giving her the last sensation she needed to fall over the cliff into oblivion.

Randy followed right behind her.

As Nicki's eyes fluttered shut, she thought she heard Randy mumble, "I love you, Nicki."

Despite the pounding of her heart, Nicki drifted off to a troubled sleep. A short time later she woke with a start, somewhat disoriented.

Had she dreamed making love with Randy that last time? The creamy residue on her thigh said she didn't dream it. With a start, she remembered there were no more condoms.

Oh my God. She made love to Randy without protection.

What the hell was wrong with her? She couldn't afford to take a chance like that.

Her heart pounded in her chest.

She eased out of the bed then practically sprinted to the bathroom. There was just enough moonlight coming through the window to allow her to see without turning on the lamp. She used the toilet then grabbed a washcloth and washed away as much as she could. At the sink, she leaned on the counter and looked into the mirror.

It had been a mistake to think she could get intimate with Randy and keep her heart out of it. She loved him. She had never stopped. But she couldn't afford to repeat history.

She splashed water on her face to clear her thoughts.

She needed to get away. The roads should be clear enough that she could go home.

Resolved, she brushed her teeth then quietly made her way into the other bedroom. In the dark, she dressed warmly and stuffed the rest of her things into her bag. After digging out her keys, she tiptoed into the den.

It didn't take long to gather the paintings and the other trinkets and return them to the writing chest. She left it in the foyer near the door.

With her bag in hand, she headed out into the cold to start her car. As she slipped behind the wheel, she said a prayer it would start. It took a couple of attempts, but it roared to life. Nicki sighed with relief.

She adjusted the heater and made sure none of her warning lights had come on. When she got out she inspected her tires then the area around the car to make sure all of the branches and debris were out of the way.

Randy had done a great job of cutting up and removing the tree, so there shouldn't have been any problem. But it didn't hurt to double-check. Satisfied her path was clear, she returned to the house.

As she repacked her cooler, Randy came into the kitchen. "What are you doing?"

Damn. She had hoped she could sneak out without having to say anything. "I was just grabbing my coffee and my cooler."

"Are you leaving? Right now?"

"Yeah." She snapped the lid closed on her cooler and picked it up by the handles. "I couldn't sleep so I thought I'd go before traffic got too crazy."

He narrowed his gaze. "You weren't even going to say good-bye, were you?"

"I, uh…" She swallowed nervously. "No. I thought it might be better."

He took a step closer. "For who? You?"

"For both of us." She lifted her chin. "Look, I had a nice time with you this weekend. And I'm glad we had a chance to reconnect. But you have a business to grow and I have a couple of paintings to research. So let's just end this on a good note and maybe we'll see each other at the next big family gathering."

She impressed herself by being able to say all of that with a straight face even though her heart screamed in protest.

"No."

Nicki blinked in confusion. "No?"

He crossed his arms over his chest. "No."

"What do you mean by no? That you don't want to end it on a good note? Or that you won't be at any more family gatherings?"

"No to all of it. I don't want you to leave and I don't want to end it on any kind of note."

"You can't mean that. We haven't seen each other in almost a decade. You have a life in Chicago. I have one in Springfield. And we have a whole lot of history between us. A lot of unresolved hurt and feelings." She brushed past him and set her cooler next to the writing chest. "I think you're lonely, just like me, and we had this time to ourselves, and somehow those feelings got mixed up with the memories we had together of our time here at the cabin." She shook her head. "It isn't real. And it won't last past you driving across that state line."

"You're wrong."

He marched to where she stood and grabbed her by the arms. "I know what I feel for you. What I've always felt for you. I knew it before I came, but it took seeing you again to admit it to myself. Making love to you solidified it." He lifted her chin, forcing her look at him. "And make no mistake about it, it was making love."

She closed her eyes so she couldn't see the earnest look on his face. "No." She shook her head, freeing herself from his touch. "It was just sex. It was just closure. That's all."

He frowned. "How can you say that?"

"Because that's all it can be. Because if you try to make it more then I'll want more, and I don't think that you can give more."

"How do you know that?"

"Stop." She waved him off. "Just stop. I need to go." She wrapped her scarf around her neck and made sure her gloves were in her pocket. Even if her car wasn't warm yet, it would be in a few miles.

"Stay, please. We'll talk. I'll even keep my hands to myself."

"No. I can't." She sniffed back the tears that threatened to spill. "I just can't, Randy. I'm sorry."

She scooped up the chest and her cooler and all but ran out the door. With a prayer of thanks for her foresight to pop the trunk earlier, she dropped the chest in and slammed the lid closed. Then she jumped into the driver's seat and pulled away.

The last thing she saw in her rearview mirror was Randy standing in the doorway. Something told her that image would haunt her for the rest of her life.

CHAPTER TWENTY-SEVEN

Getting up the drive to the highway had been tricky, but Nicki's panic overrode even her better sense. Her little car slid a few times, but the uneven gravel beneath the snow gave her extra traction.

Once she was on the main road, she drove as fast as she could with the conditions. Randy tried to call at least four times before she even made it across the lake but she didn't answer.

What would she say?

"Good-bye" made her throat feel as if it were swelling shut. But he couldn't possibly want her. Not for the long haul. This weekend had been closure and nothing more.

She couldn't afford to let it be more than that.

No matter how many times she told herself she only had a day or two before her period started, she couldn't let go of the fear that she might have gotten pregnant.

Going home to an empty apartment and stewing over it wouldn't help. All she'd do is binge on wine and chocolate chip cookies and eventually give in and pick up when Randy called. No good would come of that.

Steve would keep her honest, though.

She looked at the time. It was still a little early, but he would probably be in the office already. She dialed his number and waited for him to pick up.

"Marketing, this is Steve."

"Hey."

"Hey yourself. How's it going?"

"Actually, I left early this morning. I'm almost back to Springfield."

"That was quick. I thought you wouldn't be home until later

tonight or maybe even tomorrow."

"Yeah, well, I wanted to have time to do some research on the paintings before I returned to the office tomorrow."

"Really?" Steve asked in disbelief. "You left a cozy cabin, complete with a hunky ex-flame, to come home to an empty apartment and work? Are you out of your mind?"

"Probably. But I just couldn't stay. I had to get out of there."

"Why? What happened?"

The more she thought about her reasons for leaving, the stupider she felt. "Nothing."

"Nothing happened between you and the hunky ex? You two have been there, alone, for four days, and you expect me to believe that nothing happened?"

"Well, no, I mean…" Nicki stuttered. "What I mean is, yes, something happened," she added under her breath, "several times, actually." Without knowing quite how to explain what she was feeling, she blurted, "But, I just couldn't stay up there any longer."

"Oh." Steve said, sounding disappointed. "So the sex wasn't as good as you remembered it, huh?"

"No, no, no. That's not it at all. The sex was great." She cleared her throat. "I mean—"

Steve perked up. "Reaaaally," he drawled. "So, let me see if I got this straight. Your ex shows up. The guy you've been pining for as long as I've known you. You hit the sack with him. The sex is great but you went running out of there as soon as the roads cleared. Did I get that right?"

"Well, yeah. Sorta," she mumbled.

"Sister, what is wrong with you?"

"I don't know," she whined into the phone. "I'm so confused."

"Okay. Where are you and when do you think you'll hit town?"

"Maybe in another half hour."

"You want me to meet you at your place?"

"No. I don't want you to get into any trouble by taking off for me."

"Oh, please. I worked my ass off this weekend on the presentation. Which went great, by the way. So, I'm due for some time off."

"That's great, Steve! Do you think you'll get that promotion?"

"It looks pretty good. Mr. Tennison said he wanted to meet with me next week to go over some of the data and let me know next steps."

"That sounds promising, doesn't it?"

"You bet. Marcie is green with envy. That's just a little perk."

Nicki laughed. Marcie had been a pain in Steve's butt since he started working there, so she was glad to see him get an edge on her.

"Okay, so, what do you want me to do to make you feel better, sis?"

"Well, if you're sure you can take off, I would appreciate the company." She sighed into the phone. "I feel the need for some junk food."

"I can stop for a couple of things on the way. You in the mood for a healthy dose of Rocky Road?"

"Definitely Rocky Road. Maybe even some cherry chocolate chip, too."

"Damn. You are down, aren't you?"

"I don't know what I'm feeling right now, Steve." Her voice broke.

"Oh, don't you get all sniffly on me. You know you'll just get me started, and I need to get out of here before I get all blubbery. So just hang on until you get home and then you can cry and snot all over me and I won't say a peep about it. And if that man of yours has done something bad, we'll get out your fabric scraps and make a voodoo doll. Okay?"

She wiped her nose on her sleeve. "You're the best."

"I know. Now if I'm gonna play hooky for the rest of the day, I need to finish up a couple of things. I'll see you at your place in a bit."

"Okay." Nicki disconnected from the call and breathed a sigh of relief. Before she could set the phone down, it vibrated in her hand.

Ed. Huh. In no mood to deal with him, Nicki ignored his call. At least it hadn't been Randy. She couldn't avoid his calls much longer. Eventually she would give in and answer. She just didn't know what to say yet.

Maybe after crying on Steve's shoulder and drowning herself in junk food, she'd have the answers she needed.

It was worth a try.

She turned on her MP3 player and drove the rest of the way with the music to one of her favorite rock bands blaring through her speakers. Steve often teased her that he didn't know how she could still hear after years of playing her music too loud. But she didn't even want to hear the buzz of her phone in case Randy called again.

When she reached her apartment complex she parked in her usual spot. It was nice having a maintenance guy who kept the lot cleared of ice and snow each time they got bad weather. She slipped her phone into her coat pocket, grabbed her bag, and headed to the elevator. When she reached her door she put her key in the dead bolt and turned. For some reason the key met no resistance. She frowned. Surely she hadn't forgotten to lock it. She hadn't been in that big of a hurry when she'd left that morning.

The door handle offered no resistance either.

She pushed the door open and looked inside with caution. Perhaps she was just being an alarmist. When she stepped around the corner into the living room her breath caught in her chest. Her bookshelves had been ransacked. Cushions on her couch were out of place. The light in her bedroom had been left on and she could see things scattered on the floor.

It looked as if someone had a party but didn't invite her.

Her phone vibrated in her pocket, spurring her to back up and leave the apartment. She turned to dart through the door but found her way blocked.

Ed.

God, could someone more annoying have shown up?

He pulled a small gun from his pocket and motioned for her to step back. "Get back in there."

Nicki's thoughts came to a screeching halt. "What is going on here?"

"Where is the painting?" he demanded.

"The what?" She frowned. Trying to be as inconspicuous as possible, she clicked what she hoped was the talk button on her phone to answer the incoming call that still buzzed in her pocket. Maybe whoever it was would hear the conversation.

"The painting. The Monet. I want it. Now."

"But... I don't..." She narrowed her eyes. "What Monet?"

"The one you told Bob about. Hand it over *now*," he insisted.

"Ed, I don't know what you're talking about."

He shook the gun in her face. "Do not push me right now. I know you found a Monet and I want it. If you hand it over without any fuss, I'll let you go. I may have to tie you up so I have some time to get away, but that won't be so bad. Better than dead. Which is exactly what you're going to be if you don't start cooperating."

"Okay, seriously, Ed. I don't know that the painting is a Monet for sure. That's what I tried to tell Bob on the phone. I found a painting that looks a lot like something Monet would have done but I don't know it is for sure."

His face turned red. "You're the art expert. Do you expect me to believe that you wouldn't know the difference?"

She shook her head. "Not enough to declare an undocumented piece a missing masterpiece."

"Bullshit. Let me see it."

She sighed. "It's out in the car."

"You're lying."

She waved to the bag she had dropped after entering the apartment. "See for yourself. That's the only bag I took with me. The chest is still out in the car."

"Your car is too small to hold a chest." He aimed the gun at her heart. "I knew you were lying."

"Not a dresser kind of chest, you idiot. A writing chest." Even as the words left her lips, she knew she shouldn't have called the crazy man with the gun an idiot.

His nostrils flared and his eyes narrowed in warning. "I. Am not. An idiot."

She had to bite her tongue to keep from saying anything sarcastic. "Sorry," she mumbled. "Is Yvonne in on this, too? I knew she didn't like me, but I didn't think either of you were thieves." Under her breath she added, "Unless you count her trying to steal my show, that is."

"Other than being part of the reason I need the Monet, she has nothing to do with this."

Nicki frowned. "How can she be part of the reason but have nothing to do with it?"

"She has very expensive tastes. She likes the best of everything." He sniffed. "Even though neither of us can afford it."

"So this isn't about the show?"

"The show? You mean *Art at Dark*?" Ed laughed. "I don't give a damn about the show. That's between you and her. In all honesty, I wouldn't care if they took it off the air. No one watches it anyway."

"That's not true. We get lots of letters."

"So what?" He waved the gun around. "You have a prime segment time between the weather and the local news. Of course it has a lot of viewers. But none of that matters." He pointed the gun at her again. "Just tell me where the damn painting is."

"I already told you. It's in the car."

His lips pressed together and his face turned a darker shade of red. If he were a cartoon character, steam would have been coming out of his ears.

"Fine. Here's what we're going to do. We're going down to your car together. And we're going to get this chest and you're going to show me the painting. Then we're going to put the chest into my car and we're going to drive to my place. Got it?"

"No." She folded her arms in front of her.

"What do you mean no? I have the gun, so that means you do exactly what I say." The nasal whine made him sound like a spoiled child.

"I'm not going anywhere with you, Ed. If you want that painting, I'll give you my keys and you can go get it yourself. I'm staying right here."

Using the hand that held the gun, he punched her in the side of her face.

The impact knocked her off balance and the pain very nearly sent her to her knees. She pressed a hand to her cheek.

"You will do what I tell you or you will regret it."

Oh, how she wished she were a man. A big man. One with years of boxing experience. Because right now, she could very well imagine knocking Ed's teeth loose.

A headache pounded through her skull and reminded her that she shouldn't call him an asshole.

"What do you think you're going to do with the painting anyway, Ed? It will take months, maybe even years to confirm whether or not it's a Monet. If you're expecting to cash it in somewhere and make millions, you're wrong. No one will touch it until it's been researched and properly documented."

For the first time Ed appeared unsure of himself. He quickly shook it off. "You're just saying that."

"No, I'm—"

Ed jabbed the gun into her chest. "Shut up. Just. Shut. Up."

If it hadn't already been sore, she would have bitten her lip. The urge to tell him what she thought of him warred with her sense of self-preservation.

"You're going to take me down to your car and you aren't going to say another word. Got it?" He motioned to the door with the gun. "Now move."

She resisted the urge to give him a go-to-hell look and did as he said. Out on the landing outside her apartment she scanned the walkway for fellow residents, even though it was questionable whether they would be a help or a hindrance right now.

When they reached the elevators, she gestured to the door marked Stairway. "I usually take the stairs but this is your show."

"Use the elevator."

She pressed the button to call the elevator. When the doors opened her mouth fell open at the sight that greeted her.

CHAPTER TWENTY-EIGHT

Randy's mind bombarded him with images of Nicki being attacked in her apartment. Each one worse than the last. By the time he parked his car and found her building he was in a near frenzy and ready to do battle with the Hulk.

He took the elevator to the third floor like Charlotte had instructed. The doors opened to let him out and he found Nicki waiting there with a man.

Randy scanned her from head to toe. Relief that she was alive and mostly unhurt flooded his system. The red mark on her face, however, made him gnash his teeth. He forced a neutral expression on his face when he switched his gaze to the man.

This had to be Ed.

"Hey, there you are," Randy said with more nicety than he felt. "I was just coming to see if you were home yet."

Nicki gaped then glanced at Ed. "Uh… I…"

"You said you wanted to go bowling with us so I came to pick you up." Randy held out his hand. "Are you ready?"

Her eyes were huge in her head and he thought she had turned a little pale. Hopefully she would figure out the call she picked up while in the apartment had been from him and that he knew what was going on.

"She's busy. Something came up at work." Ed brushed Randy's hand aside and ushered her into the waiting elevator.

Randy followed. "Aren't you still on vacation?"

"Well, sort of." Nicki glanced at Ed.

Ed's hand twitched in his pocket. That had to be a gun. Why else would Nicki leave with him?

"But it's okay," she reassured him. "They need me at the

station. And I'm sure they'll reimburse me a few vacation hours, won't you, Ed?"

The doors opened and Ed prompted her to move. "Sure. Whatever."

As they entered the parking garage Ed turned to Randy. "Look. We're in a bit of hurry, so why don't you run along? I'm sure she'll call you if she's still interested."

"You okay with that, Nicki?" Randy asked.

She nodded once. "It's just something I need to take care of. It'll be fine."

The fake half smile she gave him made his stomach turn.

In the distance, a siren wailed as it drew closer. Ed stiffened. "Let's go. Now. You drive."

"You in a rush?" Randy asked, stalling them.

"Yes, as a matter of fact, we are." Ed propelled Nicki farther into the garage.

"Well, you at least need to get the bag you left at the cabin from my car," Randy suggested to Nicki.

Nicki's cheeks turned pink. "I, uh… I was in a bit of a hurry when I left. I can get it from you later, though."

"What is it?" Ed demanded, looking back and forth between them. "What did you leave?"

"I doubt that's any of your business." Some of Randy's friendly demeanor slipped.

Nicki dug in her purse. "Here." She offered Ed her keys. "My car is right over there. I'll just go grab my bag from Randy's car. You get what you need from the trunk, okay?"

The sirens grew louder. Randy prayed Ed would take her offering and keep this from getting worse.

"No." Ed pulled the gun from his pocket and pointed it at them. "You wanted to play hero, so you can just come along." He jerked the gun toward the garage. "Let's go."

The look Nicki gave him said, "What now?"

He shrugged and took her by the elbow. "Where's your car?"

"Over there." She pointed to an area to their right.

"I assume your bags are in the trunk?" Randy asked.

"Yes." In a whisper she added, "You shouldn't have come."

His jaw tensed. "There was no other option."

"Shut up. Both of you," Ed barked.

Randy shot Ed a look that promised retribution as soon as he got that gun away from him.

"Don't get any ideas," she whispered. She gestured to her dented car. "Here. Now what?"

Ed pointed to the rear of the car. "Open the trunk. I want to see the painting before we leave."

Nicki went to the back. Randy stayed where he was.

Ed shooed him along. "You, too."

Randy gave Ed another dark look then went to stand next to Nicki.

She opened the trunk and pointed to the wooden chest. "There. Just take it and go, Ed. You don't need us."

He glanced in and stepped back. "Open it."

Nicki looked at Randy. He shrugged.

"Hurry," Ed demanded as the sirens grew louder.

Nicki opened the lid and pulled the small painting out. She unwrapped the tissue paper, exposing the painting, and left the precious cargo on top. When she stepped away, Randy tugged her to the side, placing himself between her and Ed.

"Is that what this is all about? A painting?" Randy asked.

The sirens kept getting louder. Anyone could tell they were headed in their direction. Randy assumed it would be the police. Charlotte had said she would call them as soon as they hung up.

Nicki tugged on Randy's sleeve. "Let him have it. Ed, just go."

"I don't think so." Ed gestured with the gun. "Both of you into the car. I'll get in the back. You drive."

"Where do you think you're going to take us?" Randy stopped Nicki from getting into the car.

"What difference does it make?" Ed asked. "Just get in."

"No." Randy pushed Nicki aside then lunged for Ed.

He managed to land one solid punch to Ed's nose but didn't deflect Ed's gun hand fast enough. The gun went off and Randy dropped to his knees in pain. He grabbed his side where he would swear he had been stabbed by a red-hot poker. He struggled to focus on Ed and what was happening around him, but his vision swam, making it hard to focus on anything.

He heard Nicki on the other side of the car where he had pushed her. Hopefully she had been out of the way when the gun went off.

A few feet away Ed clutched his nose. Blood dripped from beneath his fingers. He used the bumper of the other car to stand then scrambled to his feet and lunged in Nicki's direction.

Randy grabbed Ed's ankle but the movement cost him. Nausea rolled through his belly but at least he had managed to trip Ed and keep him from reaching Nicki.

Nicki dove for the gun and leveled it on Ed.

"Ed, stop. I don't want to shoot you, but believe me, I will." Without taking her eyes off Ed, she scooted closer. "Randy, are you okay?"

"Yeah. Mostly," Randy groaned. His ears were ringing too loud to tell if the police had arrived based on the sirens, but the flashing lights in his peripheral were a welcome sight. He kept his quickly dimming vision on Nicki.

"What's wrong?" Nicki asked, her voice laden with fear.

"It's fine," he lied. "Don't worry about me. Just make sure dickhead doesn't do anything stupid."

An officer shouted, "Police!"

Nicki yelled to be sure they heard her. "Over here!"

"Drop your weapon!"

With one hand in the air, she put the gun on the ground and slid it toward the police. She was smart enough to do it on the side of the car away from Ed, then she put her other hand in the air.

"My friend has been shot. Please hurry." Her voice broke when she looked down at his belly.

He said a prayer of thanks that she had stayed where she was even though he could tell by her expression she wanted to help him.

Two officers moved cautiously in their direction. "Get on the ground."

She did as they ordered but didn't take her eyes off him. Tears streamed down her cheeks. "Please help him. He's been shot."

"Oh, thank God," Ed said. "Officers these two were trying to steal my property. Arrest them."

"What?" Nicki's mouth hung open.

Despite the pain in his side, Randy could have kicked Ed in the teeth at that moment.

"Both of you shut up and don't move," the officer barked.

"Sir, are you okay?" one of the officers asked.

"I'm not sure." Randy looked down at his side. When he saw the blood, his head swam.

"You've been shot?" the officer asked.

"Yeah."

The other officer spoke into his radio and called for an ambulance.

"Who shot you, sir?"

Randy flicked his thumb at Ed. "This dickhead."

"Ambulance on the way," the other officer remarked.

"All of you put your hands behind your back."

"But they attacked me," Ed protested.

"Sir, hands behind your back."

Ed sat up and pointed. "It's them, not me. Arrest them!"

"Sir, get back on the ground and put your hands behind your back. Now."

At that moment, Randy wasn't sure Ed was capable of complying. He'd acted crazy enough that it wouldn't surprise him if he ignored the police. But Ed finally did what they were saying.

A little of his tension eased when they snapped a pair of cuffs on Ed.

Unfortunately the knot came back when they snapped cuffs on Nicki. "Can I sit next to him," she tipped her head toward Randy, "while we wait for the ambulance?"

"Sorry, no. Not until we straighten this out." The officer wrote something in his notebook.

The officer closest to him locked the cuffs on then checked his wound. He mumbled something about getting a bandage.

"Are you okay, Randy?" Nicki pleaded.

"To be honest, I'm feeling a little woozy."

The officer who cuffed him exchanged a look with his partner. "The ambulance should be here pretty quick."

"Can I help, officer?" A woman stepped out of the crowd that had gathered just outside the garage. "I'm a nurse."

"Yes. That would be great." The officer gestured to Randy. "Gunshot wound. Bleeding pretty bad."

The woman squatted next to Randy and checked his wound. "Do you have a kit?" she asked the officer. "I need something to stop the bleeding and I'd like to check his blood pressure."

The officer went to his car and returned with a small first-aid bag.

As the nurse did what she could to stop the blood flow, Randy looked in Nicki's direction to see how she was holding up. Her skin was pale and she barely noticed when the second officer came to ask her questions.

As he watched Nicki being questioned, his vision darkened and the ringing in his ears grew louder. The weakness pressing down on him was winning. He just needed a minute. He wanted to tell Nicki he loved her.

Maybe he could after he rested for a bit.

CHAPTER TWENTY-NINE

"What is your name?" the officer asked.

"Nicole Cartwright." Her answer came automatically. She never took her eyes off Randy and the paramedics who were treating him.

"You work at Channel Eleven, don't you?"

"Yeah."

"My wife loves that art show of yours. She's always trying to get me to take her to see stuff you've talked about."

Finally she looked up at the officer. "Oh. I'm glad she likes it." She attempted to give him a little smile.

"So, tell me how you got involved in this, and who is this guy?" The officer pointed to Ed.

"That's Ed. He's one of the station managers."

"He said you two were trying to steal something of his."

She shook her head. "He's lying. It isn't his. The painting belongs to my grandmother."

"A painting? What's so special about it?"

She took a deep breath. "My grandmother said her mother bought it in France while vacationing there. It's been stored for over fifty years. I just got it out of the attic this weekend and wanted to have it inspected and appraised." She shrugged. "And quite frankly, I had hoped to do a special report on it."

He grunted. "And where is this painting?"

She tipped her head toward the trunk of her car. "In there."

He looked inside. "That little thing?" He shook his head. "Start at the beginning and tell me your version of what happened."

As she related the day's events with the officer, she watched Randy being loaded into the ambulance. Before they closed the doors, she asked, "I don't suppose there's any way I could go with him, is there?"

"I'm afraid not. We have to get to the bottom of this first."

"Can I call his grandmother?"

The officer shook his head. "The hospital will get a hold of his family."

"Where's my granddaughter?" Charlotte's voice echoed through the parking structure. "Nicki? Are you here?"

One of the other officers spoke up. "Ma'am, this is a police scene. We need for you to stay back."

"I'm the one who called you people. I want to know where my granddaughter is. Nicki?"

The officer who had been questioning her asked, "Is that your grandmother?"

A lump formed in her throat when she heard the concern in her grandmother's voice. "Yes."

"I'll go talk to her," he offered. "But you need to stay here."

Nicki nodded. She couldn't have spoken anyway. She was too choked up.

Randy hadn't moved at all when they loaded him into the ambulance. And the way the paramedics had fussed over him, unwrapping packages and attaching IVs, worried her even more.

He couldn't die. Surely fate wouldn't be so cruel.

The officer speaking to her grandmother pointed in her direction and then to the ambulance. Charlotte pulled out her cell phone and nodded as she punched in a number. Most likely she was calling Randy's grandmother. Steve joined Nana and nodded at whatever the officer said.

Steve caught her gaze and gave her a quick wave. Nicki forced a weak smile.

The officer headed back in her direction. "She's calling your friend's family but said she'd wait here until you were finished."

"Thank you." Nicki blinked away her tears.

Eventually they were all taken to the police department for more questions and paperwork.

All in all, the process took longer than she liked but finally they let her go. As promised, Steve and her grandmother were waiting for her. Good thing, because it would not have been safe for her to drive in her state of mind.

"Have you heard anything about Randy?" Nicki asked as soon

as she reached them.

"He's out of surgery and resting but they're keeping an eye on him," Nana Charlotte reported.

"He had to have surgery?" The tears she'd managed to keep at bay during the ordeal flowed freely. "What happened?"

Steve chimed in. "He was shot. The bullet went through his intestine, so they had to repair the damage and close up the wounds."

Nicki's knees went weak. Steve caught her and kept her from crumpling to the ground.

Charlotte added, "They said everything went well but he needed to be monitored for a few days for infection." She crinkled her nose. "Apparently a lot of nasty things get loose when that part of the body gets a hole or two."

"Poor Randy," Nicki moaned. "How is Rosie doing?"

"Better now that they know Randy is going to be fine."

"Good." Nicki pulled her coat on. "So, can you take me to the hospital?"

Steve pulled the keys out of his pocket and shook them. "We figured you'd want to go right away."

Nicki nodded. "I do."

Charlotte took her hand as they hurried to the car. "I know you want to see Randy, but I have to insist that you eat something on the way. You probably haven't had anything all day, have you?"

Nicki wrinkled her nose. "I'm not sure my stomach could tolerate much."

"I know, but at least eat a little bit of something," Charlotte insisted.

Steve clicked the key fob to unlock the car doors. "What about just a milkshake and some fries?"

Charlotte and Nicki both slid into a seat and fastened their seat belts while Randy got behind the wheel.

"All right," Nicki reluctantly agreed. "As long as we can get something quick."

Even though they came from her favorite fast-food joint, the fries tasted like cardboard, but it did put something in her stomach other than bad coffee.

Her grandmother and Steve chatted as they drove to the hospital, but Nicki paid very little attention to what they were saying. All she could think about was Randy and whether or not he was okay.

When they arrived at the hospital, Charlotte led the way to a waiting room. They spoke to Randy's grandmother and grandfather then Nicki excused herself to check on Randy.

She slipped into his room and shut the door behind her as quietly as possible. Machines flashed an assortment of numbers in a slow, steady rhythm proclaiming all was well.

She walked to the bed and drank in the sight.

An IV bag hung from the pole at the corner. Wires snaked into the opening of his hospital gown and another led to the monitor attached to his finger.

The entire time she was being questioned at the police station, her mind had been consumed by the possibility that she might never see Randy again. Not breaking down into a puddle of tears had taken every ounce of control she possessed.

Now that she was here and could see how close he came to dying, all because of her, her control gave out. Tears fell as she drew closer.

Unable to help herself, she brushed the lock of hair aside that had fallen onto his forehead.

At her touch, his eyes opened.

"Hey." She gave him a watery smile.

"Hey yourself." His voice came out hoarse.

"How are you feeling?"

He grimaced. "A little sore."

The dam inside her broke. "I'm so sorry. It's my fault that you got shot. If I hadn't told Bob about the painting then Ed wouldn't have found out about it and he wouldn't have tried to steal it. Then you wouldn't have gotten shot and you wouldn't be here and you wouldn't have almost died." She took a ragged breath. "You almost died." She shook her head. "You can't die, Randy. Please don't die."

His hand closed around hers. "I'm not dying."

She hiccupped. "But you almost did."

"I don't think it was that bad."

"Yes, it was." She couldn't stop her blubbering. "You were unconscious when they put you in the ambulance. I thought I would never see you again. And I couldn't stand that."

He smiled and squeezed her hand. "Does that mean you would have missed me?"

"Of course I would have missed you. How can you even ask that?"

He raised a brow. "As I recall, you were the one who left without saying good-bye. That doesn't sound like someone who cares whether or not they see someone again."

Using her sleeve, she wiped her eyes. "I was upset and I panicked."

"What upset you? I thought things were going well."

"They were. Really well. But I knew you'd be leaving and I didn't want to experience that again." She looked down into her lap and whispered, "I barely lived through it the last time."

"So you decided to leave first."

She bit her lip and nodded.

He motioned for her hand. When she placed her palm against his, he threaded his fingers through hers. "I understand." He brought their joined hands to his lips and kissed the back of hers.

The gentleness of his touch made her sniffle again.

"Nicki, did it ever occur to you that I wasn't going to tell you good-bye?"

"Yes. That's why I left."

He smiled. "No, I meant I was planning to tell you I wanted to continue to see you."

She frowned. "But you live in Chicago and I live here."

"That's true. But there's something you don't know."

She raised her brow in question.

"Before I left we received a request to bid on a project here in Springfield. Vince and I discussed it and agreed to pursue the opportunity. I planned to stay after the party to meet with the client. We need more information before we can begin our proposal."

A small glimmer of hope blossomed in her chest. "You mean you'd be coming here on business more often?"

"Actually, Vince and I were thinking it would be the perfect opportunity to expand and open another office."

"In Springfield?"

"Yes."

Her mouth fell open.

"Look. I know I hurt you before. And I can't tell you enough how sorry I am. I screwed up and I hurt you. I wouldn't blame you if you told me there was no chance we could ever be together." He squeezed her hand. "But I would really, really, really like another chance to make it up to you. To show you how good we could be together. The way we should have been if I hadn't been a dumbass."

Tears pooled in her eyes again.

"Something has been missing in my life, but until I saw you at the cabin I didn't know what." He kissed her hand again. "No woman has ever measured up to you and they never will. Will you please give me a chance to make the last eight years up to you?"

"You mean you want us to be together? As a real couple?"

"Yes. As a real couple." He grinned. "Whatever that is." He tugged her closer. "Nicki, I love you. I never stopped loving you, and I want you in my life again. Call it whatever you want. As long as it means you and I see each other and that we can be together in the most intimate way possible."

She smiled, but doubt remained latched in place. "Are you sure it's not the drugs talking?"

"They may have helped me say things I might not have otherwise said, but that doesn't mean I don't feel them."

The door to his room opened, drawing their attention.

"Ah. You're awake. Good." The nurse checked the machine next to the bed then patted his arm. "How are you feeling?"

"Okay." Randy didn't sound as if he was being totally honest.

"It's time for your meds. If you want a little more time with your visitor, I can come back in a bit." The nurse looked at Nicki. "They'll make him sleepy."

"Does that mean I need to leave?"

Randy tightened his grip on her hand.

"That's up to you two. I'm just warning you that he'll most likely fall asleep," she grinned, "so don't take it personal."

Nicki smiled. "I'll try not to."

The nurse finished her inspection of his IV port. "I need to check on a couple more patients, so I'll come back in a few minutes."

"Thank you," Randy said.

"They say sleep is the best thing you can do to heal the body," Nicki told him after the nurse left.

"I know, but I haven't even been able to ask if you're all right. Pop told me the police were releasing you but not what happened."

"I'm fine." She covered their hands with her free one. "Thanks to you." Then she shook her finger at him. "But you'll be hearing what I think of you taking on a crazy person with a gun later on. That can wait until you're better, though."

He chuckled. "I'm sure I'll be hearing it from Gram, too."

She made a harrumphing sound. "Serves you right."

"So what did the police say?" he asked, redirecting her line of thought.

"I can tell you the details later when you're feeling better. But the bottom line is that Ed confessed. I think it had something to do with the surveillance footage they received from the apartment complex. That and Bob's statement."

"So no charges brought against you?"

"No."

"Good. I figured not when I woke up and the cuffs were gone."

Nicki shuddered. "God, I hated that. I'm not sure I will ever get over that part. You were shot and bleeding but they still put you in cuffs."

"It's standard operating procedure. I get it. They had no idea who the good guy was, or the bad guy."

"I know. I do, too, but it killed me to not be able to do anything to help you."

He pulled her onto the bed and wrapped his arms around her. "It's okay. It's over now."

"Thank God." She sniffled against his chest. "But I have to confess that if Ed wasn't in jail right now, I'd be tempted to shoot him in the same exact spot that you were shot. Only I wouldn't call anyone to come help him."

Randy chuckled. "You don't mean that."

She lifted her head. "Yes, I do. I may not in a few days, after I've had a chance to calm down and process everything, but right now, I do."

"A bit bloodthirsty, don't you think?"

She laid her head on his chest again. "Maybe." She sighed. "I'm glad you're okay."

"I'm glad you're okay, too."

"When do you think you'll be able to go home?"

He shrugged. "I think they said three or four days as long as I didn't show signs of an infection."

"And how long until I can give you a proper thank-you by licking all of your fun parts?"

He made choking sounds. "Uh… Hopefully less than that."
She smiled. "I'll hold you to that."

EPILOGUE

"And we're out. Good job, Nicole."

"Thanks, Mike." Nicki handed her microphone to the intern helping Mike, the cameraman. "Now I'm going to find my date."

The intern pointed to the group of men hovering near the bar. "I think I saw him over there with Mr. Chapman."

"Thanks."

Nicki touched her hair and set her sights on the man who had snuck into her life and back into her heart. So far that she could no longer imagine living without him.

Halfway to her destination her path became blocked by a familiar cloud of hot-pink satin and floral perfume.

"Yvonne." Nicki forced a smile. "How are you enjoying the evening?"

"Actually, it's better than I thought it would be." She waved one well-manicured hand about the room. "The caterers did a wonderful job, the location couldn't be better, and everyone who's anyone came. Should make a great feature story."

"I'm glad you think so." This time, her smile was genuine. "What time do you go on?"

"Depends how long the auction lasts."

Nicki nodded.

"Oh, and I wanted to tell you that your friend Steve is simply adorable. I don't know why you haven't brought him around before."

"I guess I never thought he'd enjoy himself at any of our events."

"Well it's a shame." Yvonne patted her arm. "Speak of the devil. I'm going to go catch up with him and see what he thinks of

Lynette Vanguard's dress." She leaned closer. "Personally, I think it looks like she pulled it right out of her thirteen-year-old daughter's closet but didn't let the seams out."

Nicki cringed. "You may be right." She touched Yvonne's arm. "Oh, I wanted to tell you thank you for handling that, er... enthusiastic fan for me. Bob told me you found out who was sending the flowers and creepy notes and that you'd talked to him personally."

Yvonne lifted one glittering shoulder in a half shrug. "I had a similar situation a few years ago. Poor guy only wanted to get my attention. He just didn't know how to do it without looking like a pervert." She sighed. "Some guys just don't have enough social experience to express themselves properly."

"How did you find out who was sending them?"

Yvonne leaned closer and whispered, "I know the owner of the flower shop."

"They told you who it was?"

"No." Her blonde curls bounced when she shook her head. "I didn't ask her to betray customer confidence. I simply asked her to pass along a message that included my office number the next time he came in."

Nicki crinkled her nose. "What did you say when he called?"

"Oh, the usual PR nonsense. I thanked him for being a loyal viewer and told him we really appreciated his support but pointed out that receiving multiple bouquets and notes from fans can make our employees and their families uncomfortable." She waved one hand through the air. "He apologized and said he wouldn't send any more. So, problem solved!"

"I hope he understood and didn't get his feelings hurt."

"Nah. I promised to send him one of our promo pictures signed by the entire morning crew. He was thrilled."

"Well, good. I'm glad. And thank you for taking care of it."

"You're welcome." She leaned and looked past Nicki. "Now, I need to catch up to that friend of yours before Mrs. Silverman gets her mitts on him. If she does, he'll never get loose."

"By all means, go save Steve."

Yvonne wiggled her fingers over her shoulder as she sauntered away.

Nicki shook her head and said a prayer that Steve didn't mind Yvonne's clinging attentions. The man was well on his way to being nominated a saint.

After Randy had thanked him for being there to support her during her worst moments, the two of them had reached some kind of agreement and even a level of friendship. Now Steve was quickly winning over Yvonne. Taming the beast, so to speak.

It was remarkable and only made her love her dear friend more.

When she refocused on her original destination, she found Randy watching her. A shiver ran through her body, knowing what the look in his eye meant.

He liked her dress. But he liked that she wore nothing beneath it even more. It made her glad she had whispered that secret in his ear as they got out of the car when they arrived.

She couldn't wait until they were alone. There was a sexy trick she read about in a magazine that she wanted to try. It promised to make any man's eyes roll back in his head.

Might be a little risky to try on the drive home but after would be fair game. She loved making him squirm as much as she loved it when he returned the favor.

Randy met her halfway. "Are you finished with your spot?" His voice sent a fresh wave of heat spiraling through her body.

"Um hmm." She tipped her head to one side. "Have I told you how sexy you are in a tux?"

He chuckled as he slipped his hand around to the small of her back. "If formal wear does it for you then I may have to invest in another one so I can wear it on the weekends."

The kiss he pressed against the side of her neck sent tingles all the way down to her toes. "As long as I can take it off you."

"Definitely."

Randy raised his head and looked around. "I guess it's still too early for me to drag you away?"

"Afraid so."

"Dammit," he mumbled.

Nicki grinned then leaned closer to whisper, "But if you make a sweep of the room with me, I'll see if we can sneak out once the auction starts."

"Deal." He grasped her elbow and propelled her toward a group of guests.

They made small talk and assured themselves that everyone was enjoying their evening. Just as they finished a full circuit around the room, the announcement came that the art auction would soon begin. Guests began filing into the larger ballroom where the live auction would be held.

Nicki looked up at Randy with a question in her eye.

"Are you sure you don't want to stay for the auction?" he asked.

"No. There's nothing I planned to buy. And Mr. Hartsford let me look to my heart's content after our interview last week."

"You sweet-talked him, didn't you?"

Nicki grinned. "Maybe a little."

He nodded toward the exit. "If you're sure you won't be missed, I certainly wouldn't complain about leaving early so I can get my hands on your delectable body."

She stopped him by putting one hand on his chest. "As much as I love that idea, what about you? Weren't you supposed to talk with David Kaiser about your ideas for his project? You said it would be huge for you and Vince if you could land that deal."

Randy pulled her hand off his chest and kissed her palm. "He found me while you were getting set up."

"So how did it go?"

"Good. If I read him correctly, I think we have a good shot at landing the job. David was open to all of my ideas and said he'd like to get together with us sometime next week."

"That's wonderful! So you really might be able to justify moving here?"

He wrapped one arm around her waist and pulled her closer. "I can already justify it. I want to move here because I want to be near you. And Gram and Pop. You're the only one who thinks that's not a good enough reason."

"I know, I know. We've talked about this several times. I just want to make sure you're sure before you do anything rash."

"I love you, Nicki. One of these days you're going to believe me."

Tears pooled in her eyes. "I know you do. I love you, too."

He pulled her closer into a hug. "And maybe one of these days you'll not cry when I tell you I love you."

She chuckled then murmured against his chest. "That may take a while."

"As long as you love me back, we'll be just fine."

With her arms around his waist, she squeezed. "Let's get out of here. I suddenly have an urge to show you just how much."

"Far be it from me to deny your request." He kissed the top of her head then stepped out of her embrace. He draped one arm around her shoulders and led the way from the gallery. "Hey, I didn't get a chance to ask if you were happy with how they displayed your grandmother's painting."

"I think they did a good job with it. It's hard to display smaller works like that. And since we don't know the value yet, it's a judgment call on how much security is needed."

They notified the valet they were ready to leave then retrieved their coats from the coatroom. When they stepped outside to get into Randy's vehicle, the cold night air triggered goose bumps on her bare flesh. It even managed to reach the dampness that had been pooling between her legs. She instantly regretted giving him a hard time for using the valet service. In the past she'd seen it as a frivolity, but it was nice to walk only a few steps then get into an already warm vehicle.

Especially since neither her dress nor her shoes provided much protection from the cold.

Not that Randy couldn't warm her up again.

He proved he could, even with one hand on the wheel. Without taking his eyes off the road, he eased her skirt up and located her clit. His firm strokes and teasing flicks had her racing to orgasm before they exited the highway.

When they reached her apartment complex, Randy let her out near the elevator then parked the car. He could be quite the gentleman.

"You should have gone up," Randy said when he found her by the elevator. "You didn't need to wait for me."

"I know." She sank into the warmth of his arms. "I wanted to wait for you." Despite her efforts, her teeth chattered when she spoke.

"Let's get upstairs so we can both get warm again."

Randy used his own key to unlock the door to her apartment. All evidence of Ed's break-in had been erased thanks to her building's superintendent. She'd gone a step further and installed a security system.

After closing and locking the door, Randy pulled her into his arms and kissed her thoroughly. She melted against his frame, loving the way their bodies fit. The cold quickly dissipated, leaving only a burning need for him.

His hand moved down her back, slipped beneath the edge of

her dress, then cupped her bare butt. If she didn't already know, the firm line of his erection pressed against her belly would have given away his arousal.

He murmured against her lips, "It was killing me knowing you were walking around without panties." He slipped his hand between their bodies and down to her pussy. The touch of his finger on her clit made her quiver with anticipation. "You have no idea how hard it was to keep my hands off you." He teased her folds and bud and made her knees weak.

Before she fell too far under his spell, she stopped him. "There's something I've wanted to do all evening."

His brow furrowed. "What's that?"

"This." She unfastened the top two buttons of Randy's shirt and licked the small indention at the base of his throat. "And this." She ran her hand down his chest and abs then cupped him through his perfectly pressed black slacks. Keeping her eyes locked on his, she lowered his zipper and adjusted his briefs so she could grasp his bare cock. Using a firm grip, she stroked him a couple of times to ensure she had his attention. In a near whisper she told him, "I read something in a magazine the other day that promised to make a guy's eyes roll back in his head. I want to try it on you."

His cock twitched and his pupils dilated, but otherwise he maintained a cool façade. "All right."

She gave him a teasing smile. "Come with me." Without releasing her hold on his erection, she led him to the bedroom. She flipped the light on as she passed and encouraged him to stand next to the bed. She took a step back. "I don't want to get anything," she looked meaningfully at his crotch, "on my dress. So would you mind helping me with my zipper?"

She lifted her hair then presented her back to him.

He slowly lowered the tab then kissed the spot between her shoulder blades.

A delicious shiver raced down her spine. She let the dress fall to the floor then turned to face him.

He raked her from head to toe with a hungry glint. "Damn. You are beautiful." He reached for her but she held up one hand to stop him.

"I want to do this," she reminded him.

One side of his mouth lifted. "All right."

She dropped to her knees at his feet and looked up. Starting at his ankles, she ran her hands up the front of his legs. When she reached his waist she unbuckled his belt and worked the button of his pants free.

She tipped her head back and looked up at his face. A rush of power coursed through her, knowing she held his complete attention. She licked her lips and leaned forward so she could blow a puff of warm breath down the length of his cock. It jumped in response.

Using one hand, she grasped his erection and held him steady as she slowly leaned closer. Using only the tip of her tongue, she traced circles around the head then followed the trail down to the base where her fingers gripped him. She made several quick licks back up to the tip then with a gulp took him all the way into her mouth.

He hissed and grabbed a handful of hair on the back of her head. Another zing of heat whipped through her, knowing she had damaged his considerable control.

When he eased his grip on her head she continued but with slower licks. Her free hand alternated between caressing his balls and touching her own breasts. As soon as she sensed him relaxing she sucked him all the way into her mouth again. Once again his breath halted and he gripped her hair.

He only allowed her to tease him like that one more time before he pulled her up off the floor. "Enough." His lips crashed onto hers as he backed her into the edge of the bed. They tumbled onto the comforter and struggled to move his clothing out of the way.

Thankfully her brain hadn't become overrun by her hormones and she was able to remind him of one last detail. "Condom."

"Shit." He reached into the drawer next to the bed and pulled one out. "I'll be glad when your pills kick in so we don't have to use these anymore." Using his teeth, he tore the foil package open and rolled the membrane into place.

"Me, too," she said.

They both groaned when he sank into her heat.

"I hope you're close," he murmured.

She wiggled, trying to get him to move. "If you'll just touch that one spot…"

"I'll do more than that." He pulled out of her body then flipped her over onto her belly. Using his knee, he spread her legs then once again buried himself in her.

He reached around to the front and found her clit. The first touch made her stiffen from sensory overload, but it quickly passed. She pushed back to meet his thrusts. It felt so good she had to bite her lip to keep from begging him for more.

"Nicki," he groaned between clenched teeth.

"I—" She gasped through broken breaths. Something about the change of his angle was the last sensation she needed. "Oh God." The dam broke and a tidal wave of pleasure washed through her. Somewhere in the haze of sensation she felt Randy collapse against her back, and they both fell forward onto the mattress.

They lay with limbs entwined as their breathing returned to normal.

"Your tux is going to get wrinkled," Nicki mumbled.

"I don't care."

She smiled and tried to roll over but he held her in place. It required too much effort to struggle, so instead she snuggled closer. Not that she had far to go.

When her heart finally stopped beating against her chest, she elbowed him to encourage him to roll over. He grunted and gave her enough room to move. She turned and wrapped her arm around his waist.

Her fingers automatically searched out the bullet wound near his hip. She traced circles around the puckered flesh and recalled the events of the last few weeks. Their weekend at the cabin. Ed's attack. Her new job at the station. And Randy's partial move to Springfield.

"I love you," she said.

Randy froze. "Do you realize that's the first time you've said it first?"

She nodded. "Yeah."

He wrapped his other arm around her and squeezed. "You know you're not getting rid of me now, right?"

She smiled against his chest. "Hmmm. I can live with that."

The End

~ Save an author by leaving a review ~

ABOUT THE AUTHOR

Liana Garson loves to read romance—the hotter the better. When she isn't writing or cleaning up cat hair, she loves to crochet and watch Big Bang Theory re-runs. Somehow she still manages to make it into the office on a regular basis.

Find Liana on the web at:

Website - www.lianagarson.com
Facebook - https://www.facebook.com/LianaGarson.Author/
Twitter - @Liana_Garson
Email – Liana.Garson.author@gmail.com

Signup for Liana's newsletter at:
https://landing.mailerlite.com/webforms/landing/a3p2b5

OTHER BOOKS BY LIANA GARSON

Risky Business
Down to Business
Working It All Out
Loss of Control